Acclaim For the Work of MAX ALLAN COLLINS!

"Crime fiction aficionados are in for a treat...a neo-pulp noir classic."

—*Chicago Tribune*

"No one can twist you through a maze with as much intensity and suspense as Max Allan Collins."

—*Clive Cussler*

"Collins never misses a beat...All the stand-up pleasures of dime-store pulp with a beguiling level of complexity."

—*Booklist*

"Collins has an outwardly artless style that conceals a great deal of art."

—*New York Times Book Review*

"Max Allan Collins is the closest thing we have to a 21st-century Mickey Spillane and...will please any fan of old-school, hardboiled crime fiction."

—*This Week*

"A suspenseful, wild night's ride [from] one of the finest writers of crime fiction that the U.S. has produced."

—*Book Reporter*

"This book is about as perfect a page turner as you'll find."

—*Library Journal*

"Bristling with suspense and sexuality, this book is a welcome addition to the Hard Case Crime library."

—*Publishers Weekly*

"A total delight…fast, surprising, and well-told."
—*Deadly Pleasures*

"Strong and compelling reading."
—*Ellery Queen's Mystery Magazine*

"Max Allan Collins [is] like no other writer."
—*Andrew Vachss*

"Collins breaks out a really good one, knocking over the hard-boiled competition (Parker and Leonard for sure, maybe even Puzo) with a one-two punch: a feisty storyline told bittersweet and wry…nice and taut…the book is unputdownable. Never done better."
—*Kirkus Reviews*

"Rippling with brutal violence and surprising sexuality…I savored every turn."
—*Bookgasm*

"Masterful."
—*Jeffery Deaver*

"Collins has a gift for creating low-life believable characters …a sharply focused action story that keeps the reader guessing till the slam-bang ending. A consummate thriller from one of the new masters of the genre."
—*Atlanta Journal Constitution*

"For fans of the hardboiled crime novel…this is powerful and highly enjoyable reading, fast moving and very, very tough."
—*Cleveland Plain Dealer*

"Entertaining…full of colorful characters…a stirring conclusion."
—*Detroit Free Press*

"Collins makes it sound as though it really happened."

—*New York Daily News*

"An exceptional storyteller."

—*San Diego Union Tribune*

"Collins' witty, hard-boiled prose would make Raymond Chandler proud."

—*Entertainment Weekly*

"Violent and volatile and packed with sexuality...classic pulp fiction."

—*USA Today*

"As cool as an Eskimo Pie on a hot summer day and as sharp as a Ginsu knife."

—*Milwaukee Journal Sentinel*

"Nobody does it better than Max Allan Collins."

—*John Lutz*

"For seventeen years," Spade said, "Gutman tried to track that black bird down. It became his life's obsession. Finally he discovered it was in possession of an exiled Russian general in Constantinople name of Kemidov, who apparently had no idea of the actual worth of the falcon."

"What is the actual worth?" Bryan asked.

"If you can believe Gutman," Spade said, "who was a championship windbag, remember, it could bring in as much as two million."

Bryan's eyes popped behind the lenses and the black ribbon danced. "Dollars?"

Spade shrugged. "Maybe. Could be pounds. Gutman threw figures around generously."

Bryan's eyes were narrowed now. "Does this damned jeweled falcon even really exist?" the D.A. asked, shaking his head.

"Hell if I know." Spade got to his feet. "Does it matter, if people are killing over it...?"

HARD CASE CRIME BOOKS BY MAX ALLAN COLLINS:

QUARRY
QUARRY'S LIST
QUARRY'S DEAL
QUARRY'S CUT
QUARRY'S VOTE
THE LAST QUARRY
THE FIRST QUARRY
QUARRY IN THE MIDDLE
QUARRY'S EX
THE WRONG QUARRY
QUARRY'S CHOICE
QUARRY IN THE BLACK
QUARRY'S CLIMAX
QUARRY'S WAR *(graphic novel)*
KILLING QUARRY
QUARRY'S BLOOD
QUARRY'S RETURN

SKIM DEEP
TWO FOR THE MONEY
DOUBLE DOWN
TOUGH TENDER
MAD MONEY

DEADLY BELOVED
SEDUCTION OF THE INNOCENT
RETURN OF THE MALTESE FALCON

DEAD STREET *(with Mickey Spillane)*
THE CONSUMMATA *(with Mickey Spillane)*
MIKE HAMMER: THE NIGHT I DIED
(graphic novel with Mickey Spillane)

RETURN of the MALTESE FALCON

by **Max Allan Collins**

A HARD CASE CRIME BOOK
(HCC-167)
First Hard Case Crime edition: January 2026

Published by
Titan Books
A division of Titan Publishing Group Ltd
144 Southwark Street
London SE1 0UP

in collaboration with Winterfall LLC

Print edition ISBN 978-1-83541-487-3
E-book ISBN 978-0-83541-488-0

Design direction by Max Phillips
www.signalfoundry.com

Typeset by Swordsmith Productions

Printed and bound in the United States

EU RP:
eucomply OÜ Pärnu mnt 139b-14 11317 - Tallinn, Estonia
hello@eucompliancepartner.com,+3375690241

Visit us on the web at www.HardCaseCrime.com

In memory of
Robert J. Randisi
the private eye's friend

"Don't be too sure I'm as crooked
as I'm supposed to be.
That kind of reputation might be good business
—bringing in high-priced jobs and
making it easier to deal with the enemy."

Sam Spade

in Dashiell Hammett's *The Maltese Falcon*

DECEMBER
1928
San Francisco

CHAPTER ONE
The Petite Client

Samuel Spade, leaning back in his swivel-chair, studied the modest pine tree that might have sprouted tinsel-trimmed from where his late partner's desk had till lately stood.

Less than two weeks ago, that partner, Miles Archer, was shot and killed. A recent client of the Spade & Archer detective agency, a woman calling herself Brigid O'Shaughnessy among other names, currently resided in a cell in San Francisco County Jail #1, charged with Archer's murder. Spade had put her there.

The private detective's vaguely satanic face—with its V's of heavy dark eyebrows over horizontal yellow-grey eyes, beaky hawk nose, and pointed chin—appeared at repose. Only a crease between those eyebrows bore any suggestion he might be mulling something.

His crisp brown suit with brown-and-yellow tie complemented dark blond hair, if fitting the slightly irregular six-foot frame less well due to wide sloping shoulders, narrow waist and long dancer's legs. He and his office looked moderately successful though the amber desktop was spare, home only to a small clock, a brass ashtray, a spiral pad with #2 pencil, and a leather-framed green blotter. Morning sun passing through the window cast SPADE upon the floor, only hints of the ARCHER remaining on the glass, tidbits not quite razored off.

Effie Perine, his secretary, came in from the outer office, boyishly pretty and sunburned despite temperatures in the forties this time of year. Her notebook and pencil were in hand. The lanky, tawny-haired girl was twenty-three and he was ten years older.

She said: "I hope you don't mind the tree, Sam."

"It fills the space for now."

The secretary's low heels clacked toward him over the linoleum flooring; her thin tan woolen dress clung to her. "I can add some decorations if you like," she said. "Just tinsel looks sad somehow."

"No, it's festive enough." He looked at her. "Anything on the docket today?"

"You hate it."

She was still on the subject of the tree.

"It's fine. What's on the docket?"

Effie Perine sighed and sat in the client's chair, legs crossed primly. Her habit was to perch on the edge of his desk, but she hadn't done that lately. Right now the entire desk was between them. Among other things.

"A Miss Smith called and made an appointment," she said stiffly. "No referral."

He said: "You're sure it wasn't Miss Jones?"

She drew in a breath. "With the bad publicity we've had lately, I didn't feel I could be too particular about what clients we took."

"Ah." His tone was light. "*Your* name is on the door now, is it?" He gestured over his shoulder. "Plenty of room for it on the window, now that Miles is gone."

The young woman's chin came up. "That's not fair, Sam. The *Call* made you look very bad last week and you know it. That nasty Lt. Dundy and pompous District Attorney gave out some most unflattering quotes."

"Remind me to bust out crying." He shrugged the slope of his shoulders. "Anyway, that kind of thing only builds business."

Something like a pout formed on pretty, lightly rouged lips. "From people named Smith or Jones, perhaps."

From his suitcoat pocket he took a sack of Bull Durham

tobacco. A packet of brown rolling papers already waited on the desk. "Look, precious, if you're fed up with me, and you want me to write you a letter of recommendation to prospective employers, just say so."

She dodged this suggestion with a question. "How is Mr. Archer's widow holding up? This time of year can be difficult. After a tragedy and all."

His expression was soft with hard eyes in it. "I'm not seeing Iva socially any longer. We had what you might call a falling out."

The secretary brightened, momentarily, then said, "I may be out of line saying, Sam, but I think that's for the best. You *were* a suspect in her husband's murder, after all."

"You're right," he said with a smile, "you *are* out of line."

She swallowed, closed her notepad, stood and swished out in a flurry of silk stockings and thin fabric, shutting the inner office door with not quite a slam. Soon the sound of her typing came through, louder than the norm.

Spade chuckled to himself as his thick fingers carefully dropped tan flakes down into a curve of rolling paper until each end appeared equal, with slightly less between them. His thumbs rolled the paper's inner edge down, then up and under the outer edge where his forefingers could press it over, thumbs and fingers guiding the cylinder of paper at either end. He licked the flap, left forefinger and thumb pinching one end while the right forefinger and thumb smoothed a damp seam and twisted that end before settling one tip of the roll-your-own cigarette between Spade's lips.

This ritual, which he repeated numerous times in any given day, he appeared to find soothing. It may have aided his thinking, or helped him avoid thinking at all. With his pigskin-and-nickel lighter, he set fire to the far tip.

Effie Perine poked her head in. "She's here. You'll probably like her."

"Oh?"

"She's young and she's female. It's Miss Smith, by the way. Not Jones."

The secretary ducked back out and, before disappearing into the outer office, gave a perfunctory nod to the blonde in a tan cloche hat who slipped in. Barely out of her teens if that, Miss Smith was pale and petite though she filled out her attire admirably; her white-collared brown tunic-style blouse and below-the-knee skirt went well with bright golden-brown eyes almost too big for the heart-shaped face. Her small hands were in off-white calfskin wrist-hugging gloves with which she hugged a modest matching purse.

For a moment Spade stared at her. Then he said: "Rhea Gutman. I didn't know you at first."

She acknowledged that with a small smile and smaller nod, while Spade—after depositing his cigarette smoldering in the ashtray—came around to guide her into the oaken client's chair opposite his desk.

Rhea Gutman said, with what seemed to be genuine embarrassment, "I was rather a fright when you saw me last."

"If you'll forgive my bluntness," Spade said pleasantly, "that was a ruse."

"My late father's doing," she said. "But he did give me a mild dose of whatever that stuff was to help me mimic a drug-induced stupor. You were actually a gentleman, helping me walk it off."

"I didn't exactly believe the stupor, but felt it best to let it play out."

"Yes. To keep you busy while your office, and then your apartment, were searched. My father and his associates hoped to find a...certain item...and avoid having to deal with you further."

"I had that 'item' salted safely away, not that it mattered in the end." Spade tossed the words carelessly aside. "After all, that supposedly priceless Maltese falcon was a phony."

She seemed about to reply but then didn't.

Spade filled the silence emotionlessly. "My condolences on the death of your father."

"Thank you."

"We had our differences, but Casper Gutman was nothing if not an interesting specimen. He raised you?"

She shook her head, blonde arcs slipping past her hat to shimmer in morning sun filtering through the buff-curtained window behind him. "No, my mother did. In New York... Manhattan. They divorced when I was a child. We saw him from time to time, and he was an avuncular if only occasional presence. Mother said he was handsome and slender when they met. She'd been a waitress at the time...she still was when she passed, having worked her way to assistant manager in a nice restaurant in the theater district. She died of tuberculosis a year and a half ago, my mother."

Spade seemed to have exhausted his capacity for condolences. He said, "And your father came back into your life at that point?"

One gloved hand removed a handkerchief from the purse. "Yes. I was sixteen then. I've only recently turned eighteen. I didn't finish high school, but I certainly got an advanced education, traveling with my father. In the Orient, mostly. He said he valued me."

"I'm sure he did," Spade said ambiguously.

"He liked to show me off. Would comment on my..." She blushed, her cheeks reddening like a china doll's. "...comeliness. Introduced me to various men with whom he was doing business."

The vertical crease between Spade's brows deepened. "Was he your father or your procurer?"

Rhea Gutman swallowed and her eyes went to the handkerchief she was torturing in her lap. "I deserve that, after…the way I fooled you."

"*Tried* to fool me," he corrected.

She made herself look at him. The big golden-brown eyes begged for understanding. "My father was many things, Mr. Spade, not all of them pleasant or socially acceptable. But he was *not* his daughter's procurer. He made use of me, yes, but as a…distraction. For the men he did business with. In return I saw parts of the world, experienced things other girls my age and social class might only dream of. Fine cuisine, the best hotels, exotic locales…all of these constituted my advanced education."

Spade said: "Is that why you made an appointment to see me, Miss Gutman? To explain yourself? I assure you it's unnecessary."

Her manner became suddenly businesslike. "I came to hire you for a specific purpose, Mr. Spade. It may not appeal to you, however."

"Try me."

She shifted in her seat, her eyes on the ash of Spade's cigarette writhing in the brass tray. "I am not destitute."

"I'm relieved to hear as much."

"But neither am I…flush. What I have is the ten thousand dollars that had been found on my father at the time of his death. The police returned it to me. Ten one-thousand-dollar bills." She snapped open her purse and swapped her handkerchief for an off-white leather wallet that matched her gloves.

Spade raised a stop palm in a gentle gesture. "Let's not get ahead of ourselves, Miss Gutman. Or do you prefer 'Smith'?"

"Gutman is fine. I didn't know if you'd see me if I used my real name."

Spade smiled, tight-lipped. "I hold you no animosity for our previous encounter. The farce you and I played out was your father's doing. We each played our roles, so let's get on with the next performance."

Her eyes, sharp now, went to his face. "You really don't trust me, do you?"

He flipped a thick-fingered hand. "Trust is earned. But for the right retainer, we'll consider it earned. I do need to know what the job is."

Her sigh started from deep in her bosom. "I'm afraid it's the same job, Mr. Spade. Or that is, a job you've undertaken before."

"I'm listening."

Her words came out in an earnest rush. "My father's only legacy is the jeweled golden statuette known as the Maltese falcon. He invested heavily in its pursuit, of his time and his energy and his savings. He had been, in his day, a millionaire, at least if he was to be believed. That affluent period, at his passing, was long since over."

Spade's cigarette had burned down in the brass tray; he began to roll another, absentmindedly methodical. "I was not aware that Casper Gutman had any legal claim on the artifact."

She leaned toward Spade. "I have a bill of sale from the Russian general, Kemidov…not with me—but in the hotel safe at the Alexandria. That's where I'm staying."

One V-shaped eyebrow lifted. "Still in 12C?"

"Yes. Kemidov, it seems, was…not reliable."

"A four-flusher."

"I don't know what that is, Mr. Spade."

"A cheat. A double-crosser. A crook."

She gave several short nods. "He is certainly all of those things. Those very *unpleasant* things. Mr. Spade, my only inheritance is my father's quest for that golden bejeweled bird. Completing that quest is the only way I have of honoring him."

Spade's smile was fleeting. "I doubt, should you lay hands on it, that statuette would live on a shelf of honor in your home."

Rhea Gutman lifted her chin and lowered her eyelids. "I have no home, Mr. Spade. And you are correct that I would sell that antiquity to the highest bidder." She leaned forward in her chair. "If you can recover it for me…for my late father and me…I would make you a partner in the enterprise. A full partner."

The yellow-grey eyes narrowed. "Your father seemed to think the dingus was worth something like two million."

She blinked. "The what?"

Thick fingers brushed the air. "Dingus. Object. Thing. My guess is it may be worth well into the high thousands. Six figures, perhaps. But my experience with that…dingus…is that a lot more money is talked about than actually shows itself."

"Will you take on the job, Mr. Spade?" She got into the wallet and withdrew a thousand-dollar bill. When Spade had last seen that particular slice of currency, it had been crisp and new. Now the bill had been folded into the wallet and looked fairly shopworn. It also bore brown splotches in a few spots. She handed the bill toward him.

He took it.

"You could start by seeing Joel Cairo," she said, again businesslike, referring to an associate of her late father's who Spade had encountered more than once, including in this office. "I understand he's behind the same iron bars as the O'Shaughnessy woman."

"Well," Spade said, as he lighted up his latest roll-your-own with his lighter, "they don't share a cell. But they do share an address—the county jail."

The lighter snapped shut.

His client said, "Cairo may have leads for you. And there are rumors that the Russian general is in the States. Perhaps may even be here in San Francisco. If so, finding him might be a priority."

Spade frowned, issuing smoke that coiled like a snake. "Where did you get that information?"

"Oh, uh, the police. They were most cooperative and sympathetic."

"Uh-huh."

She scooted back her chair, arose and extended a gloved hand. "Thank you, Mr. Spade. I just knew this was the right place to come."

He shook the coolness of the leather-bound hand without rising. "Yes, this agency rather has a lock on Maltese falcon-related inquiries."

Ignoring the remark, looking very pleased with herself, Rhea Gutman went into and through the outer office and Effie Perine's typing ceased.

His secretary, coming through the inner office door with pad and pencil, threw a glance behind her just as the door onto the corridor closed.

She said to her boss, "You mind my asking what that was about?"

"Sit," he told her, and gestured to the chair that Rhea Gutman had emptied. "She warmed it up nicely for you."

Effie Perine made a face and sat. And Spade told her everything.

"That damned statue again," she said, shaking her head, tawny curls dancing. "Why are you fiddling with it? It got at least three people killed this month. And the Gutman girl isn't *that* good-looking."

"She's good-looking enough. Here." He slid the thousand-dollar bill toward his secretary like a playing card he was dealing. "Bank that on your lunch hour."

Her big brown eyes got bigger. “Good lord. I’ve never seen a bill this size. What are these stains?”

With terrible casualness, he said: “Casper Gutman’s blood.”

She dropped the bill as if it were burning.

Spade laughed. “Don’t worry, angel. It’s dry by now.”

Effie Perine shuddered. “Oh, Sam. That’s awful. That’s horrible.”

“The bank won’t mind. Put it in the agency account. How are you doing with that report for our Market Street client? I heard you typing furiously out there.”

“I’ll have it finished this afternoon. You’ve got the goods on them.”

The manager of a Market Street moving-picture theater suspected a cashier and doorman of colluding to defraud him. Spade had discovered two other employees involved. It would be up to the manager whether Spade’s information be given to the police or if the embezzling employees simply dismissed. Spade would advise the latter if full restitution was made.

“You have an appointment,” Effie Perine reminded him, “with the movie-house man first thing tomorrow.”

Spade leaned back in the swivel-chair. “I’ll come in early and go over your report and my notes. He gave us a fifty-dollar retainer and I’ll soak him for another fifty. Be well worth it for him—they’ve been picking him clean.”

She nodded and retreated back into her domain, pad and pencil in hand. Soon he could hear her typing again, with no furor now.

The next morning Spade, who usually prepared his own breakfast in his small Post Street apartment, stopped at John’s Grill on Ellis Street. He had eggs over easy, crisp bacon and light toast, with a side of sliced tomatoes. Belly warm, he strolled out into a chill foggy morning, dark grey fedora tucked down, tweed topcoat buttoned up.

At a quarter till eight A.M., Spade entered his darkened office. He hung his topcoat and hat on the coat tree near the burbling water cooler; his suit today was light grey, his shirt white with green stripes, his Florsheims brown and minorly scuffed. Effie Perine, coming in at eight-thirty, would have time to go over her report and his notes, and he would have time to make any additions or corrections.

Without turning the outer-office lights on, Spade moved into the semi-darkness of the inner office and his hand went reflexively for the light switch, which clicked but summoned no light. He was mid-frown when the blow came.

This came not from a blunt object but a forearm that shoved against Spade's lower neck and into the back of his head with considerable impact. It would have been sufficient to drop him but the unseen assailant at his back added insult to injury by taking Spade's legs out from under with a sweeping calf that came around catching the detective below the knees and toppling him. Hitting the linoleum floor face-down and hard, a stunned Spade was momentarily helpless as the assailant came down forcefully to sit on Spade's hips and begin pummeling him, big fists smashing into the detective's ribs on either side like a schoolyard bully. Then the attacker grabbed Spade by the hair and smashed his head repeatedly into the flooring.

As if the repeated bashing had woken him up rather than disoriented and pained him, Spade bucked the figure off his back and scrambled to his feet, pausing at the door jamb in dizziness for a moment; but the figure, a man in a dark business suit, slipped by, rushing out through the outer office and into the corridor.

Spade staggered a few steps in hopeless pursuit, then fell to his knees, and onto his face again. A scent of sandalwood and citrus lingered in the air and on Spade's clothes. He passed out while his nose bled a teardrop trickle.

When Spade awoke, he was in Effie Perine's desk chair in the outer office. He didn't know how she'd got him there and never asked. She was daubing his face with a cool cloth and her expression was distressed.

"What happened, darling?" she asked.

She rarely called him that—never, since he'd taken up with Iva Archer, his partner's wife.

"Somebody jumped me," he said. "In the inner office."

Her words came quick. "The light bulbs in the overhead fixture were unscrewed. Whoever it was waited for you for a while. Any idea who it was?"

"No. Maybe something to do with this falcon rearing its jeweled goddamn head again."

A cool hand caressed his cheek. "You want me to get Dr. Ames?"

Spade's doctor had an office two floors down.

"No. The only damage was to my self-esteem. Do you smell that?"

She nodded, curls bouncing. "Yes. It's a man's cologne, I think. Probably 4711 Eau de Cologne."

"How many male colognes can you recognize by sniff, angel? And how is it you can?"

"Every girl has her secrets," Effie Perine said.

"I bet she does." Spade rose from the chair and she steadied him. "Get me some aspirin, honey. After my appointment with that movie-house manager, I'm back on the falcon job."

She began to say something, thought better of it, then complied.

He made it into his office, got a bottle of Heublin Manhattan cocktail from a drawer, and poured himself a paper cup's worth. He saluted the tinsel-draped tree where his partner used to sit.

"Goddamn early in the day for it," he said to nobody between sips, "but I earned it."

CHAPTER TWO
Jailhouse Follies

After his appointment with the Market Street movie-house manager, Spade leaned back in his swivel-chair and called Sergeant Tom Polhaus at Davenport 202, the Detective Bureau number.

"In the mood for a bribe, Tom?"

Polhaus chuckled and said in his somewhat hoarse voice: "Always, Sam. What you got in mind?"

"Pickled pig's feet at the States Hof Brau."

"You're on. Noon?"

"Noon."

The restaurant, on Market Street with four streetcars and heavy auto and foot traffic out front, was a bustling affair. The two men hung up their topcoats but kept their hats on and were collected by owner/manager Big John himself, who guided them through the haze of tobacco smoke to a booth. The easygoing Polhaus sported thick ruddy features, a barrel belly and shrewd little eyes; he was as tall as the well-groomed Spade but wore a slept-in-looking suit. From a no-nonsense waiter in black with a pristine white apron, the sergeant ordered the promised pigs' feet and Spade the Jaeger schnitzel.

Over the clink of china and din of conversation, they exchanged small talk till their luncheon arrived. Tom inserted a forkful of pale bright jelly into his mouth, savored and sent it down. Then he cheerfully asked, "What's this going to cost me, Sam?"

Spade swallowed spaetzle. "There's a couple of prisoners at the county jail I want to see."

Tom's head tilted doubtfully. "Come on, Sam. That's a sheriff's department operation. You know that."

"Let's assume you have friends in high places. Or maybe low ones."

Tom cut a bite from his pig's foot but his enthusiasm had waned. "What couple of prisoners?"

Spade shrugged. "Joel Cairo and Brigid O'Shaughnessy."

Tom almost choked on his bite of pork. "Together or separate? Too bad we're already eatin' or you could bring a picnic lunch. Hell, Sam, you know you can't see either one of them birds! You're a witness in both their cases."

Spade's big shoulders rose and fell again. "Of course they'd have to be willing to see me in the first place."

"Of course!" Tom said, mocking Spade. "How else could they bribe you?"

Spade pointed with his table knife toward Tom's plate. "You're the one eating pig's feet on the arm."

The cop's chin crinkled in mild offense. "I can pay for my own meal if need be."

Spade said, "Look at it this way. If either one spills anything, it goes straight from me to you. And I'm willing to testify about whatever new I get."

Polhaus, weakening, speared a forkful of pig's foot into his thick-lipped open mouth, chewed and talked. "I don't know, Sam…"

Spade served up half a grin. "Don't you ever want to make captain, Sergeant? Or do you enjoy carrying Lt. Dundy's water?"

The big plainclothes officer gulped down one last bite of pickled pig's feet.

Then he said: "It'll cost you."

"How much?"

"One serving of apple strudel with vanilla sauce."

Spade ordered two from an aproned waiter.

*

The Hall of Justice, a wedding cake of a building built after the 1906 earthquake, dominated Kearny Street across from Portsmouth Square; behind it lurked County Jail #1, where the fourth floor was four stories high with four tiers of cells for male prisoners, the floor above accommodating female inmates in cells and dorms.

Spade rode the elevator to the third floor. Fedora in hand, he walked past the laundry with its medicinal odors and a kitchen whose aromas did not rival the Hof Brau's. At the glassed-in administrative offices, where Polhaus had called ahead for him, Spade left his topcoat and hat and put up with a thorough frisk. Since he rarely carried a gun, it was much ado about nothing. He was then escorted by a bored armed guard and deposited in a small featureless chamber where inmates generally met with legal representation or family members.

This dark box of a room was taken up almost entirely by a floor-mounted steel table to which a single shackle was attached near a similarly mounted metal chair where prisoners were, upon delivery, cuffed. Had Spade not visited this facility before, he might have been surprised to be joined in this stark spare space by a prisoner in street clothes, not jailhouse blue.

Not that Joel Cairo's standard apparel might reasonably be mistaken for "street clothes"—the prisoner, guided toward his seat by the same sour guard, wore the dandy's attire he had to Spade's office two weeks ago. Of slight build and medium height, his black hair as smooth and glossy as if painted on a doll, Cairo minced along, his black coat hugging narrow shoulders and flaring over plump hips. The green cravat, snug trousers and patent leather shoes with spats remained while the diamond-set ruby that had adorned his cravat, his yellow chamois gloves and black derby were absent.

The stone face of the guard cracked open long enough to

inform Spade he had fifteen minutes, then departed, making sure the door closed with a cell-like slam.

Shackled by his right wrist now, Cairo seemed embarrassed by his reduced circumstances, but he nonetheless found a meager smile for Spade. "Your request to see me, Mr. Spade, comes as something of a surprise."

Spade returned the scant smile. "Not an unpleasant one, I hope."

The Levantine's eyebrows went up lazily. "I mean only that our previous interactions have involved a certain amount of… shall we say, hostility on your part?"

"After you pulled a gun on me, you mean? Twice?"

Cairo cocked his head, his lips forming a disappointed kiss. "I would say, respectfully, that your response in either case was unnecessarily…I would have to say…harsh. After all, I was merely protecting myself and looking after my best interests."

Spade was rolling a cigarette. "That's fine and dandy, but I'm not about to let anybody walk in off the street and stick me up."

His expression put upon, his cheeks crimsoning, Cairo said, "And am I to forgive someone who attempted to make of me a…'fall guy,' as I believe was the crude designation of which you made use? Am I to simply…set aside that you offered me up to your criminal associates as a sacrifice to the authorities so that you and these malefactors might run free?"

Spade laughed, lighted up the cigarette. "*My* criminal associates? You mean, 'malefactors' like Gutman and your boyfriend Wilmer Cook? Anyway, Gutman couldn't run a block. Would've been fun to watch him try, give you that."

Cairo sought to regain his poise; the red drained from his face. "Let us call all of that unpleasantness ancient history."

"Let's call it last week." The cigarette in Spade's lips bobbed with his speech. "I'm not here to say 'there there, poor baby.' If they hang you, I'll be over it quick enough."

Cairo looked suddenly sick. "Then why are you here, Mr. Spade? Do you come to torment me? To satisfy your obvious sadistic streak?"

Spade grunted. "I'm back on the hunt for that goddamn bird. The genuine article this time. I'm told the Russian, Kemidov, made the switch and still has the real McCoy. If you can lead me to him, I'll give you a share of what I haul to shore."

The dark eyes narrowed. "You are pursuing this on your own volition?"

"No, I have a client."

Cairo frowned, his head making a half turn. "Who among us remains? Most are in the ground or behind iron bars."

Spade let out a stream of smoke. "My client's name is not on offer here. A man like you should appreciate my discretion."

The Levantine mulled that. Then his smile came, like sunshine after a storm. "Mr. Spade. Enough discussion of past transgressions on either of our parts. In my reduced circumstances, I welcome any civilized company, surrounded as I am here by the dregs of humanity. You and I have not always had the most friendly of relations, sir, this I freely admit…but one in my position…what is the expression? Must forgive and forget."

"Yeah. And beggars can't be choosers and it takes two to tango." Spade leaned forward, locked eyes with the Levantine. "Look, Joe—if you can lead me to Kemidov, I'll make it well worth your while."

Cairo leaned back in the metal chair as much as he could manage; his expression sickened. "My 'while,' as you put it, Mr. Spade, is worth very little, I fear. I have no funds available currently with which to mount a defense. The charge against me is, I believe it is called, felony murder…thanks to various unnecessary homicides tied to the Maltese falcon 'hunt,' as you term it. Archer, Thursby, Jacobi. Homicides of which I had no direct part. And yet I stand in the shadow of the hangman, sir."

"Sometimes life just isn't fair." Spade stubbed his cigarette out on the metal table. "There's always a public defender."

Cairo's manner went supplicant. "I would prefer paid representation. A specialist in such matters, yes? But my funds, that is the lack of which, hamper me in this pursuit. I can confirm that Kemidov is in the USA. Right here in San Francisco, in fact. But I am afraid I cannot lead you to him. He is in hiding. Where exactly, I do not know."

Spade shrugged his sloping shoulders. "Then it doesn't seem you have anything to trade."

Cairo sat forward and his eyes jumped with the potential of a better future. "But I do. I have the name and address and even telephone number of the best buyer for the bird. A wealthy private collector who will take the damnable thing off your hands, no questions asked as they say, and fill your coffers with actual coin of the realm."

"I don't have any coffers and I'm not interested in coins," Spade said, the V's of his eyebrows rising to flatten out, "but as for actual dollars...the kind your dead pal Gutman said was worth ten dollars of talk...I'm interested, all right. What finder's fee do you have in mind, Cairo?"

The Levantine's eyes lidded; his smile showed no teeth. "Twenty-five percent would seem fair, Mr. Spade."

"I bet it would. You'll take ten and like it."

"But I do not like it. Shall we say...twenty?"

"We'll say fifteen, and don't push your luck."

Cairo's nod was curt. "Done, Mr. Spade."

With his unshackled hand, Cairo gestured. "If you would like to...shake on it, as is the custom? I'm afraid you'll have to come to me to do so."

*

Escorted by a pockmarked harridan guard, and without granting the seated Spade a glance, Brigid O'Shaughnessy strode in, fluidly feminine in a belted green crepe silk dress much familiar to him. She had been wearing it on the night Gutman and the others had gathered in Spade's apartment to wait for the falcon's delivery. That was when the fat man pretended to have been shorted a thousand dollars and Spade had been compelled to take Brigid O'Shaughnessy into an adjoining room and search her.

To make her strip.

And as the supplely shapely female walked by, breasts high, legs long, hands graceful, Spade watched her with neither apparent shame nor pleasure. As Cairo had been before, she was deposited in the metal chair and her right wrist cuffed to the waiting shackle, and still she looked not at Spade, her cobalt-blue eyes affixed to a spot on the shiny metal tabletop between them where her distorted reflection shimmered.

Finally those nearly violet eyes, half-lidded and languid under long lovely lashes, lifted to look at Spade. She wore no make-up, the usual bright red lipstick which so emphasized the perfect white teeth notable in its absence, though her short red hair was perfectly curled, a nest of pretty little snakes. Perhaps the girls on the cell block played beautician to each other before a visitor came calling.

"Hello, Sam," Brigid O'Shaughnessy said in her measured alto. "Did you come to gloat?"

Emotionlessly, he said: "I took no pleasure sending you over."

"Neither did you hesitate," she observed.

Spade shook his head in a barely perceptible fashion. "Not true. And my evidence would not be enough to convict you, anyway."

They both knew fingerprints had tied her to the Webley-Fosbery .38 revolver that killed Miles Archer, and two witnesses had seen her walk with Spade's late partner into the alley where the man's corpse was found past a broken fence against a boulder with a bullet in his heart and his gun tucked under his buttoned-up topcoat.

"You told them," she said with clipped, chin-up bitterness, "that I confessed to you."

Spade waved that off. "I wouldn't have if I'd known about the forensics evidence and the two witnesses. It's a matter of self-preservation and I shouldn't have to lecture you on that subject." He shrugged. "Let's not quibble about it."

The young woman seemed to melt into the chair's hard metal, not so much defeated as aware that Spade could not be worn down by any sense of guilt.

"It's just your word against mine, anyway," she said, in a tone of self-pity.

"That's right," Spade said brightly. "Let's change the topic."

The self-pity, which may have been at least partly an act, disappeared and she gave him a sharp, animal look. "What other 'topic' is there, considering my…my limited future."

He shrugged again, just one shoulder this time. "Let's talk about that, then."

"About what?" she snapped.

"Your limited future. As I understand it, they have you on two killings—Miles Archer and your previous defender, Floyd Thursby. Two homicides make it tough. A case could easily be made that either of those men, a letch like Miles, a known killer like Thursby, could've put you in a situation where self-defense came into play."

"Yes!" she said, sitting forward, the dark blue eyes sparking. "That's exactly how it was."

He gave her a wolfish grin. "Let's not get carried away. Embrace the concept and come up with the precise circumstances on your own time, and utilizing your own vivid imagination."

Confusion rocked her and she got the same cornered-creature look he'd seen the night he turned her in.

Spade leaned forward. "My point is that once is happenstance and twice is habit. And two homicides make for a nasty damn habit."

Through her perfect little teeth she said, "Then why bring it up? You are a damned sadist, Samuel Spade."

He had begun to roll a fresh cigarette. With a good-natured smile, he said, "That's what Joel Cairo just accused me of. I don't see it, myself."

Those remarkable eyes flared. "You've seen Cairo?"

Judging by Spade's tone, they might have been discussing the weather. "I have. You're the second half of the bill. He was seated where you are not fifteen minutes ago. The seat might still be warm."

She squirmed uncomfortably. "Why on earth would you go to the trouble of visiting that…that sybarite nincompoop here?"

"That sybarite nincompoop might've been able to lead me to General Kemidov. The Russian is thought to still have possession of a certain artifact. But Cairo didn't have anything for me. Do you?"

Through that relatively short speech, the young woman had gone through an impressive range of facial expressions: surprise, interest, frustration, and finally…purpose.

"If I could lead you to the Russian," Brigid O'Shaughnessy said, eyebrows up, eyes wide, "how could it benefit me? In these dire circumstances that you helped put me in?"

Spade ignored the latter part of that and responded to the first: "You need a top defense attorney. Or have you secured one already?"

"I have not," she admitted joylessly.

Spade lighted up his rolled cigarette, then tucked his lighter away. He blew out a stream of smoke and studied it like a gypsy and her tea leaves.

Finally he said, "My attorney, Sid Wise, is the best murder man in town. If you could lead me to Kemidov, and the Maltese falcon…let's just say you could afford that kind of representation."

Brigid O'Shaughnessy seemed amused. "After all this, you're still chasing that rainbow?"

He frowned at her. "It's not a rainbow to me. It's a payday. I could give two hoots about antiquity but I'm big on what a golden statue festooned with precious gems could bring. Aren't you?"

"Once again," Brigid O'Shaughnessy said, and a mouth so terribly pretty even minus red lipstick puckered as she spoke, "I'm afraid I once again have to be a disappointment to you, Sam. I don't have the faintest idea where that bastard Kemidov might be. My preference is he be burning in hell."

"It may come to that," Spade said. He sighed. He began to rise. "Sorry to have wasted your time, precious. Though it was a pleasure seeing you again."

Coldness came over her beauty. "I'm so happy for you. Tell me, if I'm not overstepping what remains of the great love that once existed between us…are you pursuing the falcon on speculation? Or do you have a client?"

"I have a client," Spade admitted, and he sat back down.

Her eyebrows were up again but the cobalt blues were half-lidded this time. "Would it tax your code of ethics terribly to tell me who that client might be?"

A crease formed between his brows. "That's not information I generally share."

The young woman smiled, a small smile but large enough. "Perhaps you could make an exception."

"Probably not."

She curled her finger. "Come here, Sam."

"I'm fine where I am."

"Please," the young woman said. "Come here. Just for a moment. I don't have a weapon on me, after all."

"You're plenty well-armed."

Her laughter was a gentle ripple, the kind of bubbling brook a man could drown in. "I didn't think Sam Spade was afraid of much of anything or anyone. Not an innocent girl, certainly."

"Innocent is pushing it." But he was grinning now, the wolfish one again. He got to his feet and went to the summoning finger.

He looked down at her as she looked up at him and said: "You never kissed me goodbye, Sam."

She raised her face to him and the cobalt-blue eyes beckoned. He kissed her. It lasted a while.

With her free hand she touched his face. The touch of a murderess had never been lighter, sweeter. "Who hired you, Sam?"

"…Rhea Gutman."

What appeared to be genuine sadness took over her lovely features. As if sensing danger, Spade backed away. Returned to his chair, still backing up, but did not sit.

"I know," she said softly, with a tremor in her voice, "you think a hard woman lives under this soft shell. You may not be entirely wrong, Sam. But I tell you, and I speak nothing but the truth…one of my few regrets in a life worthy of many regrets is standing by while that Gutman girl got involved in all of this. She was an innocent. And I presume *is* an innocent. Her upbringing was modest and she made perfect prey for that loathsome father of hers. That sweet kid…of all the sins Casper Gutman committed, and they are many and varied…involving that innocent child in all of this greed…greed and depravity, may well be the worst. She deserves a better life. Do you intend to take advantage of her, Sam?"

In a tone peculiarly human coming from Sam Spade, he said: “No.”

“Then help her, Sam. Find the falcon and give the poor kid a fresh start on life. Somebody ought to make out on this thing… somebody besides you, Sam.”

He grinned at her but it stopped short of wolfish. “And besides *you?* What’s this about, sweetheart? You don’t seem like the type to get jailhouse religion.”

“I’m not,” she said with as honest a smile and kind an expression as she’d ever shown him. “If you really can find the Maltese falcon, and the right buyer for it, there’ll be plenty for you and that sweet kid and…for Sid Wise. Maybe you can save me from the gallows, after all, my love.”

A knock at the door announced the scarred female guard, who barged in and collected Brigid O’Shaughnessy.

Time was up.

CHAPTER THREE
The Dingus in Question

When Spade stopped to pick up his hat and topcoat at the Administrative Offices at County Jail #1, a brunette female clerk behind the counter hailed him. Spade knew her a little, having encountered her on previous visits; attractively professional in a crisp tan business suit, she gave him a smile and said, "You might stop by the District Attorney's office, while you're here. I had a call from there."

"Am I being asked," Spade said, "or summoned?"

"Call it 'asked,'" the clerk said, with friendly sarcasm, "if it makes you feel better."

"Doesn't make me feel that much better."

She flashed a smile. "Poor baby. Still, better than an actual summons."

He gave her a nod and a smile, and went out.

The Hall of Justice connected with the jail by a glassed-in sky bridge, and where it came out Spade was met by a skinny flap-eared kid wrapped up in an officiousness he was too young to have earned and a black suit a junior undertaker would have been happy to wear.

Outside the pebbled glass door to District Attorney Bryan's office, the kid collected Spade's hat and topcoat, hung them up in a nearby closet, then knocked at the door, received a "Come!" and led Spade wordlessly in.

The spaciousness of the D.A.'s inner chamber made its walls of law books and the massive mahogany desk across the room look normal-sized. Midday sun streamed in windows like swords through a magician's box, Spade walking through the dust-mote-floating streaks to the inhabitant of that chunk of a desk, the placement of which recalled a judge's bench.

The D.A. stood and gave the detective a broad smile in a suspiciously friendly manner and extended his hand across the expanse for a handshake, a gesture Spade accepted but kept brief. The detective's last visit here had been less than auspicious and this seemingly warm welcome jarred.

Shorter than Spade and square-framed, with salt-and-pepper hair and a deep-dimpled chin, Bryan greeted his guest in a resonant voice suitable for the campaign trail: "Good to see you, Spade." District Attorney Bryan was around forty-five, and rarely blinking blue eyes lurked behind black-ribboned nose glasses, which was perhaps a pretense to make him seem older. His grey three-piece tweed suit and silk tie indicated San Francisco's office holders were doing just fine.

"Thank you for stopping by," Bryan said, tamping down his orator's voice a bit.

"Yeah, well, I was in the neighborhood."

The D.A.'s soft hand gestured toward the hard chair across from him and Spade sat, resting an ankle on a knee, hands folded in his lap, his guard up but not showing.

The D.A. took his high-backed padded chair and let out air, saying, "I realize our last informal meeting left things in an, uh…a somewhat awkward position, shall we say. Even what one might call adversarial."

Spade offered Bryan half a smile. "One might call it that. But one wouldn't call it 'informal,' not with an assistant D.A. and a stenographer sitting in."

In a friendly way that possibly masked a threat, Bryan gestured with mock casualness to the four pearl buttons on the oaken box near his desk telephone. "Would you rather this meeting be witnessed and recorded? I thought perhaps we could make this conversation more..."

"Actually informal?" Spade crossed his arms. "Fine. You're throwing the party."

Bryan's sigh was as deep as it was insincere. "I'm afraid we got off onto the wrong foot recently. I am well aware I owe you a debt of thanks for delivering to the police the murderess responsible for the deaths of your partner and that Thursby character. The woman of course can also be charged with felony murder where this Captain Jacobi is concerned."

"Kind of adds insult to injury, doesn't it?"

"The law is the law, Spade."

The detective's yellow-grey eyes took on a languid look. "So I hear. I understand Gutman's gunsel got away."

Bryan reacted as if he'd been inquired about a missing bicycle. "Wilmer Cook? Gutman's gunman, who turned on his now late employer? Yes. An individual closely resembling Cook was seen boarding a bus to Spokane. The police there are obviously pursuing all leads."

"Obviously."

The D.A. lifted a document from a stack on his desk and put it back with a flip. "Of course, I've read your statement, but we'll need to be talking again before the O'Shaughnessy woman goes to trial."

The crease between Spade's eyes deepened. "Talking again? Aren't we talking now?"

Bryan said, "Perhaps we should start over. I understand that this office made certain assumptions about you, and your behavior in this falcon affair, that were on our part, *my* part...ill-conceived."

Spade conceded the point: "I wouldn't go that far. I admit

I've been known to play things too close to the vest and go by my own rules." Then the crease between his eyes deepened again. "But any assumption that I'm outright crooked misses the point."

Bryan seemed genuinely confused by this response. "What point is that, Spade?"

Spade filled his chest with air and let it out slowly. "Well, I'm in the detective trade and my partner was murdered, so naturally I needed to do something about it. Not just by cooperating with you people on that score, but handling it myself. Aren't I an officer of the court as a licensed investigator in this state?"

"You are," Bryan admitted. "In our defense…in *my* defense… my detectives learned quite easily and early on that you and your late partner were less than fast friends. That you were even rumored to be involved inappropriately with Archer's widow."

"She wasn't his widow then, but I do find it interesting to watch a prosecutor defend himself."

Spade put his feet on the floor and sat forward, leaning an elbow on the D.A.'s desk. His teeth showed as he talked and he wasn't smiling.

"Look," he said, "if every man who slept with another guy's wife killed that guy, you'd be doing a hell of a lot more business in this office than you already are."

Bryan patted the air with both hands, clearly alarmed by how this was going. "Spade…Sam, if I may…"

The detective settled back in his hard chair, his hands on his knees, his expression bland now. "Make it Mr. Spade. What can I do for you, *Mister* Bryan? Since I happen to be in the neighborhood."

The District Attorney's expression was serious but not antagonistic, as if he realized pushing his guest had not proved a productive path.

"Let's start with that, Mr. Spade," Bryan said. "Your reason for being 'in the neighborhood'—you arranged to see two inmates at the jail this afternoon, both of whom are key players in this Maltese falcon matter—specifically, the murderess and one of the gang's surviving members."

Spade flicked half a smile. "I wouldn't call it a gang. Cronies or maybe accomplices is about as far as I'd go."

"It's far enough. What did you want with them?" He raised one palm. "I don't mean this in an accusatory way."

Spade grunted a laugh. "Look, Bryan. Mr. Bryan. I know just because we're friends now and it's just the two of us, it doesn't mean anything I say can't be used against me. You might have your stenographer listening in courtesy of that gizmo on your desk, taking notes, as far as I know. Do I need to get my attorney Sid Wise in here?"

Bryan scowled at him. "Do you? Were you colluding with those two in that visitation room?"

Spade took that calmly, replying, "The last time I was here you did a song and dance about how I was somehow in league with a Chicago gambler named Dixie Monahan, who by the way I never met. The connection was Floyd Thursby, Monahan's ex-bodyguard, who by the way I also never met. What the hell is it you want from me, anyway?"

Bryan's face turned stony. "An answer to my question."

"What question is that? I forget."

The D.A.'s hands formed fists. "What did you want with Cairo and the O'Shaughnessy woman?"

"That's privileged."

Bryan pounded one of the fists and papers jumped on his desk. "How in God's name is that privileged?"

With utter casualness, Spade said, "I was talking to those two in regard to the interests of a client I represent."

"What client?"

"That's the privileged part."

"God damn you, Spade."

Again Spade leaned forward and spoke through clenched teeth. "I spelled this out to you before. My client is entitled to a certain amount of protection and secrecy. You want me to talk, put me in front of a Grand Jury or maybe a Coroner's Jury, and if my attorney advises me to talk, I'll do so. I won't like it, but I'll do it."

The detective sat back in his chair, crossed his arms.

Though his trembling was barely visible, Bryan was indeed trembling. "Spade, and never mind the goddamned 'mister,' there are things you don't know that just might change your attitude."

"I doubt it," Spade said, "but go ahead and try. What don't I know?"

With open sarcasm, Bryan said, "Miles Archer, the partner whose murder you've been trying to clear up…remember him?"

"Vaguely."

A card player showing his winning ace, Bryan offered a gloating smile. "You may not have known the late Floyd Thursby, but Archer certainly did."

Spade stayed casual. "Miles knew Thursby? Interesting. Before Brigid O'Shaughnessy came to hire us to find her sister Corrine?"

Bryan nodded several times, self-satisfied. "Archer knew Thursby, all right. But what sister?"

Spade waved that off. "Hell, she doesn't exist—that was just part of the phony yarn Brigid O'Shaughnessy sold us for two hundred dollars. But what's this about Archer and Thursby?"

"Exactly what the circumstances are," Bryan admitted, "I don't know, not yet. My investigators are looking into it. But before you and he ever partnered, Archer and Thursby had business in Chicago. Again, this may relate to that Dixie Monahan fellow, who you may not have met, but…"

"I *haven't* met him."

"...but who nonetheless is on the fringes of this entire Maltese falcon affair."

Spade threw up his hands. "That whole mess revolved around a phony item. The only Maltese falcon I ever saw, the one people were dying to get and dying over in general, was a goddamned fake."

Bryan tugged his black eyeglass ribbon with a thumb and forefinger, then, in an apparent peace-making gesture, offered Spade a cigar from a humidor on the desk. Spade declined but took this as permission to dip into his suitcoat pocket for his tobacco pouch and papers and began to roll a cigarette.

The District Attorney lighted up a cigar, puffed, then asked: "What is this thing, anyway? This so-called Maltese falcon?"

Spade licked and sealed his cigarette, then got out his lighter. "You don't know?"

Bryan exhaled fragrant cigar smoke. "Just that it's a valuable artifact these buzzards were circling."

The detective fired up his rolled cigarette, snapped his lighter shut and tucked it away. "Well, I was one of them. It has a pretty convincing pedigree, this Maltese falcon. My secretary has a cousin who teaches at the University, Ted Christy's his name. He researched it for us, and he verified everything Gutman told me, at least as much as possible."

Bryan's eyes narrowed behind the round lenses of his eyeglasses. The black ribbon wriggled like a worm. "What you know of it came from Gutman?"

"Yes. My only source."

The D.A. exhaled more smoke. "It would certainly be helpful to know what the fuss is all about, when we're trying these various cases."

"You might get that stenographer in here," Spade suggested, cocking his head. "There's a lot to it."

"Excellent thought," Bryan said, and his right forefinger touched a white button on the bank of them.

The young man who shortly entered was the same slim colorless civil servant who had written Spade's words down on the detective's last visit here. The stenographer assumed a chair to one side reserved for his purpose and quickly got the shorthand machine out of its typewriter-style case and, fingers poised, announced his readiness with a glance.

Spade spoke slowly, perhaps not for the stenog's benefit. The detective may have been digging into his trained interviewer's mind for the convoluted story he'd been asked to relay, draining it of some but not all of its romance and melodrama.

In the fifteenth century, Spade related, a gang of freebooting crusaders got chased out of Rhodes and settled in Crete, where after a time they lobbied Emperor Charles V of Spain to give them full access to the island of Malta. To acknowledge that Malta would still be under Spanish rule, the crusaders were to pay the Emperor a tribute of one living falcon a year, else the island would revert to Spanish control.

"It was symbolic," Spade said.

This gang of crusaders was pretty well-fixed with all kinds of loot they'd stolen from the Saracens—jewels, gold, silver, silks, ivory. For the first year's tribute, to emphasize their gratitude to the Spanish Emperor, they sent, rather than a live bird, a golden falcon encrusted claws-to-crown with the finest gems from their considerable coffers.

"The ship sent out to deliver this grand gift," Spade said, "got itself plundered by a big-time pirate called Barbarossa, who you may have heard of as Redbeard, operating out of Algiers."

Some hundred years later, the fabulous statuette wound up in the hands of an English adventurer named Verney in league with Algerian buccaneers. Somehow it wound up in Sicily in the possession of the king, who made a wedding present of it to his bride.

"Turned up next," Spade said, "in Spain, then in Paris, as a spoil of war. At some point it acquired a coat of black enamel to disguise its value, and just looked like a foot-high black statuette of a bird, interesting but not very. Nothing anyone would kill over."

Around twenty years ago, a Greek art dealer bought it in Paris "for peanuts" out of the shop of a rival who had no idea of the black bird's value.

"That's where Casper Gutman comes in," Spade said.

Gutman, a notorious con artist and shady dealer in antiquities, for some time had been trying to strike a price with the Greek art dealer when the man's shop was burglarized, a thorough job that seemed to indicate the thief was not aware of this particular item's enormous value.

"For seventeen years," Spade said, "Gutman tried to track that black bird down. It became his life's obsession, his unholy quest. Finally he discovered it was in possession of an exiled Russian general in Constantinople name of Kemidov, who apparently had no idea of the actual worth of the falcon."

"What *is* the actual worth?" Bryan asked, transfixed by Spade's story. The two men, smoking their cigar and cigarette respectively, might have been in a drawing room ruminating over a fascinating old yarn. The dying day out the windows added to the mood.

"If you can believe Gutman," Spade said, "who was a championship windbag, remember, it could bring in as much as two million."

Bryan's eyes popped behind the lenses and the black ribbon danced. "Dollars?"

Spade shrugged, sighed smoke. "Maybe. Could be pounds.

Gutman threw figures around generously, but I never saw more than the ten grand I got out of him that wound up with you people. Anyway, that's where the O'Shaughnessy dame and Cairo and Thursby and that whole crummy crowd come in. Some combination of those players stole the bird from the Russian or maybe O'Shaughnessy seduced him out of it. I wasn't around for any of that. You getting this, son?"

The stenographer, startled to be directly spoken to, said, "Certainly am, Mr. Spade."

"Good. This is tricky enough without having to repeat anything."

Bryan's eyes were narrowed now. "That's everything you know?"

"Well, Cairo got jailed somewhere along the way," Spade said, turning over a hand. "Likely betrayed by O'Shaughnessy, who—with another accomplice; yes, our favorite bad penny, Floyd Thursby—fled to Hong Kong with the falcon. The woman entrusted the dingus to Captain Jacobi, probably another seduction subject, who slow-boated it here while O'Shaughnessy and Thursby took a faster one."

Bryan's expression remained narrow-eyed. "When you say 'the dingus,' do you mean the lead fake?"

Spade put his cigarette out in a glass tray on the desk. "Who can say? A switch could have been made, I suppose. Anyway, that's all I know."

"Does this damned jeweled falcon even really exist?" the D.A. asked, shaking his head.

"Hell if I know." Spade got to his feet and stretched. It had been a long meeting. "Does it matter, if people are killing over it?"

CHAPTER FOUR
Widow's Weeds

As Spade came back in after his visit to County Jail #1 and the Hall of Justice, a smug but not smiling Effie Perine said from behind her desk, "Iva called while you were out."

"I told her not to call here anymore." Spade hung up his hat and topcoat on the coat tree where it shared half a pebbled-glass-and-wood wall with the water cooler.

The young woman's big brown eyes got bigger. "Oh, I know, but she says this is business. You're to stop by this evening, no particular time. At your convenience. She's like an all-night diner."

Spade said, "Let's not be catty, precious," but he was smiling back at her as he slipped a hip onto the edge of her desk. "Iva should know the terms of my partnership with Miles better than anybody. But it's okay."

"Is it?"

He nodded. "I do need to talk to her."

"You said you were out from under that," his secretary reminded him with a frown.

If the double entendre registered on him, it didn't show. "Actually, Iva is right."

Effie Perine's response was an almost perfect red-lipstick "Oh?"

"This *is* business, angel."

"Funny business? Monkey business?"

He shifted off her desk and headed into his inner office to conclude his day. "Just business, angel."

*

After grabbing a lamb chop dinner at John's Grill, Spade took a streetcar to Nob Hill. He stepped off into an evening as clear and pleasant as the night Miles Archer's murder had been foggy and cold; he kept his topcoat unbuttoned, which if Miles had done the same, Spade's partner might not have gotten taken out so easily in Burritt Alley two weeks before.

Archer had resided on the top floor of a seven-story apartment house on the corner of Bush and Jones where similar structures stood shoulder to shoulder, their nearly even lines and gingerbread faces broken by bay windows and fire escapes above sidewalks and storefronts. Iva Archer, whose late parents had left her the building and its income, was still living there, of course. A hint was the black wreath in her window.

A Filipino boy in a red uniform took Spade up in the elevator; the kid seemed bored, not getting much business in a building this size this time of night. The elevator opened onto a modest seventh-floor vestibule shared by a modern table and lamp and a corner potted plant atop a narrow knickknack rack. Spade pressed the button set in the unmarked door's frame and the buzz elicited an almost immediate response.

Iva Archer, blonde, blue-eyed and painfully pretty, buxomly well-built and perhaps three years younger than Spade, answered the buzzer in a black satin nightgown belted over a lacy black negligee that peeked out knowingly.

"Still in mourning, I see," Spade said.

"Oh, Sam," she said with a chagrined little smile, and took him by the arm and pulled him inside. "You can be so bad."

"I get that, time to time."

She took his hat and placed it on a little table near the door. They were in a modern living room, well-appointed in pale green, beige and pastel pink, with two overstuffed chairs and a matching sofa arranged around a fireplace with a wide blond-wood frame that hugged the wall and an electric heater in its firebox. A mirror over the nonexistent mantel shelf increased the sense of size of the place. The blackness of Iva's nightwear made a stark exclamation point out of her in the soft understatement of the room.

Iva led him to the comfy sofa and unbelted her nightgown, providing a too-casual look at the lacy affair beneath. She crossed shapely bare legs. The invitation to carnality stopped just short of being engraved.

"Effie said you wanted to talk about business," Spade said as he made a cigarette. A low-slung modern coffee table that might have fallen off a zeppelin provided an ashtray.

"Yes," Iva said, the red-nailed fingers of her delicate hands folded in her lap with a modesty her attire belied. "I don't know what that Effie Perine told you. We both know how she feels about me. She seems to relish making trouble, but I told her this would be a friendly meeting."

Spade fired up the cigarette with his lighter, snapped it shut, put it away. "Effie didn't tell me much of anything. Why don't you tell me what you have in mind? Miles and I had a contract that spelled everything out. Not sure what there is to discuss."

"Basically I wanted to tell you," Iva said, cocking her head a little, "I have no intention of causing trouble."

"Always good to know."

"Yes. Yes, it is."

"Our partnership agreement, Miles and mine," Spade said, "was for three years at the end of which either of us could go our separate ways if we chose. We were in the third year and I would have pulled the plug very soon. I think you know that."

When she nodded, her Marcelled hair bounced. "I do. But I suppose we should face the difficulties presented when one of the partners passes before the end of those three years."

Spade shook his head. "No, it's spelled out. My attorney, Sid Wise, handled it, and if the contract is among Miles' papers, you should already know that I'm to share with you a third of anything the agency brings in, until the three years are up."

"Well, that seems fair," Iva said. "Even generous." This seemed to end the business discussion. "Could I get you something to drink?"

"All right. Rum and Coca-Cola?"

"Rum and Coca-Cola," she said and her moist red smile caught light from somewhere and winked at him.

Spade watched her rise and go to a liquor cart and make his drink and a matching one for herself. She wore black high-heel slippers on small feet and moved with a swish of negligee and lace. In the pastel room, the blackness of her nightwear was startling.

"And what if this art object turns up?" she asked off-handedly, pouring Bacardi in a highball glass, then the mixer, finally affixing a lime slice to its edge.

"What art object is that?" Spade asked innocently.

"Come now, Sam," she said, the red smile like a pleasant cut in her powdered face. "This jeweled thing the papers talk about."

His lips pursed in amusement. "Read about it in the *Call*, did you?"

Iva came languidly over and handed him the drink, sat beside him, not too close, and sipped at her own glass after squeezing her drink's lime slice in. "I did. Sounds fabulous. Like something out of the *Arabian Nights*." She leaned toward him conspiratorially. "Miles was killed over it, wasn't he?"

"It was related."

"Are you still…looking for it?"

"I might be."

Her mouth moved silently as if words were trying to get out. Then she said: "Would, uh…wouldn't you say I'd have a right to a share of it?"

He gave her his wolfish grin. "Is that why I'm here? You got a whiff of that bird?"

The hand with no drink in it waved at the air. "No, no, no. How can you think so little of me? Just my girlish curiosity."

"If I come across the dingus, I'll consider making it right with you. At this stage, it seems to've been nothing more than a fake and worth whatever six or eight pounds of lead might bring."

"Ah. A pity." Iva sighed. "Miles didn't leave me terribly well-fixed, you know."

"No, but your parents did." Spade rested his roll-your-own in the ashtray. He waggled a gentle finger at her. "Don't get confused about who married who for the other one's money."

"Is that all I had to offer Miles?" she asked impishly. "Just money?"

The widow placed her highball glass on a coaster on the low-slung table and leaned in and kissed him, for perhaps ten seconds, leaving some sticky red behind. Spade got a handkerchief out and cleaned off his mouth.

"You taste like a candy apple," he said.

"Want another bite?"

"No. What if it was poisoned?"

She took a moment to decide whether to be offended or not, then laughed, a ripple that started high and fell, like a brook with a little waterfall. "You're a terrible man, Samuel Spade."

"That opinion gets expressed now and then. If you want a slice of what I haul to shore where this black bird goes…if I haul in anything at all…you need to be helpful."

Her arm slipped behind him. She came closer.

"I'll do my best, Sam."

"You smell good," he admitted.

"You should recognize it. It's My Sin."

"It's somebody's."

This time he kissed her, roughly, a hand on the roundness of her back, pressing on the second skin that was satin.

Now she edged closer, her lipstick kissed away but her mouth red just the same. "What is this…art object worth, anyway?"

"You could afford to throw out all your tenants, precious, and turn this pile of bricks into a palace."

Her big blue eyes got bigger. "That doesn't sound bad at all, Sam."

He pointed a forefinger. "But you have to earn it, Iva. Nothing's free in this life."

She put her hand in his hair and messed around with it. Lazily, she asked, "What do you need from me, Sam?"

"What I always want in my business. What your late husband always wanted. Information."

The lovely woman's frown came from confusion, not irritation. "What information would I have that you might need?"

He breathed out a sigh of smoke. "About Miles. I didn't know him all that well when we went into business. His reputation, when he was with the Continental Detective Agency, was solid. Then he went into private practice and made good money doing divorce work. I never cared for that kind of thing personally, so partnering with him seemed a way to handle that type of client and bring in some income without having to do it myself."

"Miles was good with cameras," Iva said, nodding.

"I found out too late Miles and I weren't a good fit."

Her finely plucked eyebrows went up. "I knew you were planning to break off with him at the end of the year, but Miles didn't. Of course, he didn't know a lot of things."

A brief look between them indicated at least a mild sense of guilt over their relationship; but it quickly passed.

"If you've followed this in the papers," Spade said, "and from what you've picked up from me these last two weeks, the name 'Floyd Thursby' should be familiar as hell to you."

She nodded; her blonde, beautifully coiffed hair bounced again. "I know one thing."

"Yeah?"

The blue eyes narrowed to slits. "Miles was afraid of him."

"So Miles knew him, then. You don't mean knew him by reputation or anything."

"No. Not long before he went into business with you, Sam, Miles had some kind of run-in with this Floyd Thursby in Chicago."

Now Spade's eyes narrowed. "You know anything about it?"

"Usually Miles didn't tell me much about his work…but this was something big in his life, in *our* lives. The Continental Agency sent him to collect on a debt a gambler there owed to some casino boat gangsters." Her eyes tightened as if she doubted her own words. "Can that be right? Would Continental do jobs for gangsters?"

The big shoulders shrugged. "Well, those boats are legal. Anchored a few miles offshore from Long Beach and Santa Monica. State's jurisdiction only extends three miles offshore, and there's no federal law against gambling."

Her voice took on a dark color. "He told me this Thursby was a killer, very dangerous, and that Thursby had threatened him. Anyway, Miles came back empty-handed and Continental sacked him. He went into business for himself for a while, then threw in with you."

His eyes narrowed again. "Was the name of the Chicago gambler Monahan? Dixie Monahan?"

This time she shrugged. "Miles didn't say. All he said was his life was threatened by this Thursby person. Really, Sam, that's all I know. Is it helpful?"

"Might be."

A key working in the door from the vestibule caught Spade's attention, and Iva's, but she remained seated while the detective got to his feet.

A man came quickly in, stuffing some keys on a chain away in his suit pants pocket. A sturdy five eight or so, broad-shouldered, thick-necked with an almost handsome face, he wore a dark brown and well-tailored suit. The brother of Sam Spade's dead partner froze momentarily, then closed the door behind him.

"Sorry," Phil Archer said, clearly startled, "didn't mean to interrupt. I should've knocked."

"Phil," Iva said, with the ease of a woman used to covering up for herself, "you know Sam—Sam Spade, Miles' partner? He stopped by to go over a few business matters that needed tending."

Phil Archer came over to where Spade stood and extended his hand. An awkward shake followed as both men tried to figure out what to make of the situation. Spade's nostrils twitched and the V's of his eyebrows flattened out.

"Join us," Iva said to her brother-in-law, as if this were an impromptu party among friends. She gestured to an overstuffed chair opposite the sofa.

"I don't mean to interrupt," the brother said again.

"Nonsense," Iva said. "We're having drinks. Help yourself."

The new arrival did, going to the liquor cart and pouring himself a snifter of whiskey. Then he sat on the edge of the oversized chair, putting an elbow on his knee.

Iva said, "Phil's a stockbroker over in Oakland. Maybe you remember that. Anyway, he's helping me settle up Miles' estate. So many papers, so many things to go through."

Spade made an acknowledging sound in his throat.

"I'm, uh, pleased to see you, Spade," Archer's brother said. "I feel I owe you an apology."

Spade's eyes glittered, his smile stingy about showing many teeth. "Oh really? Why's that?"

"I, uh…look. I guess you know I found out about you and Iva, and it got me riled up. Was none of my business, and it embarrasses me to admit…but, after all, Miles was my only brother and, well…I'm human."

"I'm human too, as far as it goes," Spade said. "But I'm not sure that justifies you going to the police and telling them I killed your brother."

Phil Archer raised a palm. "I did not go that far. In my defense, I merely told them what I knew—that you and Iva were …involved. That Iva here had asked Miles for a divorce, although I don't believe Miles knew the why of it. But I was aware Miles was refusing to give Iva the divorce, which obviously stood in the way of you two getting married. And, well, Iva says you asked her. Proposed and all."

"Actually I didn't," Spade said.

Iva, clearly embarrassed now, shrugged and said, "It was kind of understood."

"Was it?" Spade said.

"Anyway," the brother said, "it was out of line. *I* was out of line. I hope you'll accept my apology."

"Why not?" Spade said.

"I apologize for thinking you might have killed Miles," Archer said, rather formally. "We now know you didn't. It was that ruthless woman who they have behind bars, where she belongs. So we can put all of this behind us."

"Sure we can," Spade said, and set his rum-and-Coca-Cola down on a coaster and retrieved his rolled cigarette, which had gone out. He got out his lighter again and fired it up again.

The cigarette bobbed in a corner of his mouth as he said to Iva, "I need to use the facilities. If you'll excuse me."

"Certainly," she said.

Spade knew his way around the Archer apartment. The bathroom was off a compact hall that also fed two bedrooms, the one Iva had shared with Miles Archer and a guest room. He ducked into the Archers' bedroom and saw a brown leather suitcase on a stand, more or less unpacked. He smiled to himself and the cigarette in his lips went erect.

In the bathroom he relived himself and then noted the bottle of 4711 Eau de Cologne on the bathroom counter among a few other male toiletries. This scent was what had made his nostrils twitch upon Phil Archer's entry, as he had last smelled the cologne in his office when someone attacked him there. The cologne was not one Miles Archer had used. His partner had been more of a shaving soap man.

Spade returned to the living room and remained on his feet as he put out his rolled cigarette in the ashtray and finished the rum-and-Coca-Cola in the highball glass, then returned it to its coaster.

"I'll leave you kids to it," Spade said, and ambled across the room with his hand extended as if to shake and when Phil Archer extended his similarly, Spade tightened his hand into a fist and swung it underhand into Phil Archer's groin, very hard.

The brother's cry as he doubled over, with eyes so wide they threatened to fall from their sockets, obviously amused Spade, who stood with clenched fists over the man now on his knees, as if considering what further punishment might be appropriate.

He retrieved his hat from the coffee table and seemed to enjoy Iva Archer's expression as her pretty features, distorted by popping eyes as big as her brother-in-law's, went from one man to the other, as if not sure she was seeing what she was seeing.

At the door, Spade snugged on his hat and said to the man bowing to him across the room, "I'm letting you off light, pal, since now that you've taken up with your brother's widow, you're already in for enough suffering."

Spade was out the door, closing it quick enough for its wood to take the furious pounding of Iva's fists. He didn't summon the elevator operator, instead taking the stairs. He needed to work off the rest of his rage.

Checking the watch on his wrist, Spade saw that he'd have to wait almost half an hour to catch the next streetcar. Irritated, he was looking for a cab to hail when a blow to the back of his head made the point moot.

CHAPTER FIVE
The Gunsel Again

High windows in the two-story-high ground floor of the massive worn-brick warehouse let in a layer of nighttime light from the street outside that hung and floated like a smoky dust-mote cloud well above where a man, head down, the back of his scalp matted with blood, was tied into a wooden spindle-back chair on the concrete floor.

The city outside—with its cable-car clang and motor vehicle rumble and grinding of gears and slinging of crates and bleating far-off foghorns and much closer train squeal, an ongoing cacophony occasionally punctuated by the yell of workmen—might have been a world away from this aging building. Piled on either side of this cavernous structure were used restaurant fixtures, stacks of dining chairs and tables as if every fabulous party ever held in this town had come here to die an undignified death. And yet the scent of fresh lumber piled at one end of the vast chamber keeping company with cans of paint and bags of ready-made cement and untended tool kits spoke of the remodeling underway, of the several fresh new stories being added atop this well-worn one. Something modern was rising from the ashes of yesterday, but bricks weren't ash and this wasn't yesterday. This was tonight, with Sam Spade a prisoner under a single conical lamp hanging from a distant ceiling.

Spade lifted his head and his eyes quickly focused on the two figures standing before him, perhaps five feet from where he sat and five more feet apart from each other. They were young, not much more than twenty if that, their expressions dangerously empty, their eyes particularly lifeless, little boys in big clothing and with small prospects.

At left stood a short Leprechaun-featured lad whose grey topcoat came almost to the floor, a pale yellow scarf goitering at the throat above which a round white face blossomed blankly from under a button-topped green-and-yellow plaid cap. An eight-inch piece of steel pipe was in his right hand; he was thumping the pipe rhythmically into the palm of his left.

The other youth was taller and his topcoat, black but made clownish by white buttons, was too short, as were the pants beneath, further making a comic effect out of his rolled-down socks and clodhopper work boots. His coat was buttoned to the throat and his hat was a narrow-brimmed porkpie, also black; his sunburned face was longer than Stan Laurel's if less amusing. A revolver was in his right fist and hung at his side, like a child playing cowboy in search of a holster.

From out of the darkness between them emerged a figure whose height split the difference between the other two, a figure familiar to Spade, no older than the others, with a cool pale face bearing Campbell Kid rosy cheeks and unmemorable features other than the curling eyelashes that made his small hazel eyes seem almost pretty. The neat grey cap, snugged down almost to his heavy eyebrows, the detective had seen him in before.

"Wilmer Cook," Spade said, grinning at his captor, seemingly unconcerned about his chair-confined status. "I was just starting to think I'd been shanghaied by a bunch of newsboys."

The pockets of his overcoat bulging with his trademark automatic pistols, Wilmer Cook approached Spade and stopped somewhat closer than the youthful cronies.

"Keep it up," the late Casper Gutman's bodyguard said in his low, flatly menacing voice. "Go ahead and ride me. See how it works out."

Neither the boy nor the detective spoke louder than necessary, but their words echoed anyway.

"I heard you lit out for Spokane," Spade said genially, "when it got hot for you around here. Maybe it's not too late to head that way—you have a murder rap hanging over you in this burg, after all. But they're probably watching the bus and train stations. You could always hop a freight with the hobos."

The boy lurched forward and slapped Spade with a brown-leather-gloved hand. It left a trail of blood trickling from the right corner of the detective's mouth, but Spade's only reaction was to display a tight wide smile that emphasized the satanic look of his V-motif features.

"You hit like a schoolgirl," Spade mocked, loud enough to put some ring in the echo. "Or do I flatter you?"

"Keep it up, y'goddamn lousy bastard!" the boy shouted back, and before the echo had faded he buried a fist in Spade's belly, between the clothesline bonds tying the captive to the spindle chair. "Or maybe you'd rather be picking lead out of your belly?"

Spade sat up breathing hard but still grinning. "Same cheap brand of dime novel bravado. Billy the Kid in the big city. Some gang you got here, sonny. Any of 'em weaned yet?"

The boy drew back a gloved fist, then surprised Spade by restraining himself, his clenched fingers loosening into an open palm.

The boy said, "Why don't I let my chums introduce themselves? You can see how 'weaned' they are."

The round-faced kid with the length of pipe came over and swung the thing into Spade's side. The detective winced but the blow hadn't caused any real damage—they'd left his topcoat on him and that, and the suitcoat and shirt and union suit below, were enough to cushion the blow.

Spade said to the pipe-swinger, who had taken a step back as if the bound man were a threat, “How does it work with the three of you? You sleep in bunks at the clubhouse? Or maybe in one big bed.”

The round-faced kid had turned scarlet by the end of that and stepped forward, raising the lead pipe in a fashion that suggested a head blow would follow—and Spade didn’t even have his hat to cushion any of that blow. The fedora had got lost in the shuffle.

But the boy in charge interceded.

“No, Freddie,” he said, stopping him by the arm. “I need him awake. I need to talk to him. This ain’t for the fun of it. If he goes along with us, we let him go.” The boy’s cold hazel eyes trained themselves on Spade, for whose benefit those words seemed to have been. “That’s the deal, shamus. You tell me what I want to know, this is over.”

“And *then* you’ll kill me,” Spade said affably.

The boy held up two gloved hands. “No, I’m as good as my word. You go along nice and easy and my pals and me walk, and leave you for somebody to come along in the morning and find and cut loose. This is a work site, you know. These are prosperous times. Why shouldn’t we all be in the dough?”

“Why not?” Spade leaned into his bonds. He seemed to glow in his chair under the hanging light with the young hoodlums lurking at the edges of the dark. “What do you want to know, sonny? Shall we start with the birds and the bees?”

Wilmer Cook’s grin was made out of teeth small enough to be the baby variety. “Keep it up, wise guy. I don’t have to kill you to make your life miserable.”

Spade sighed. “You might as well go ahead and kill me, son. You shot Gutman in front of witnesses. The state of California’s already going to hang you.”

The hazel eyes disappeared into confused slits. "You sound like you're askin' for it!"

"No, no." Spade shook his head and grinned some more. "Just keeping you on your toes. Tell you what. You ask me your questions and I'll tell you no lies."

The boy with hazel eyes thought about that.

He gave orders to his compatriots, at once commanding and childish, echoing in the cave of the place: "Freddie, check the front door. Eddie, check the back. Take your time."

The flunky pair nodded and shuffled off in the directions Wilmer Cook indicated.

Even with the other two gone, the ringleader moved closer to Spade, leaned in, his voice no longer echoing; he clearly didn't want his companions in on this conversation.

"Freddie and Eddie," Spade said, chuckling. "If that isn't cute as lace pants."

"Shut up."

The boy leaned in, going almost nose to nose with his prisoner.

"Word is," Wilmer Cook whispered, "you're sniffing around about the falcon again. That right?"

Keeping things confidential, Spade replied: "I have several clients who would like to know the whereabouts of that bird, yes. It's worth a dollar or two, you know."

The boy's eyes widened into alarmed marbles. "What clients?"

For a man tied in a chair, Spade seemed at ease and matter of fact in his response. "Well, as to clients, you know a couple of 'em. Joel Cairo? Brigid O'Shaughnessy?"

The boy frowned. "They're in stir."

"That's where I met with them."

The frown deepened in confusion. "They just let you in to talk to them?"

Spade grinned his mocking grin. "I find getting in is no

problem. It's the getting out that presents a challenge, at times."

The captor was still speaking in a near whisper. "You working for anybody else?"

Bound or not, Spade managed a shrug with both his shoulders. "That's privileged information. There is one other client, I can tell you that much. It's an individual who'd prefer not to have his or her name bandied about. But I don't think it's of any worry, any concern, to you."

Wilmer Cook sneered. He was close enough for Spade to smell Sen-Sen on the boy's breath. "Is that right, flatfoot?"

Spade's manner took on a friendly edge. "Why are you hanging around town, anyway? Gutman said the answer was in Constantinople. Hell, he said that as he went out the door the last time I saw him, with you part of the party. I figured the lot of you were headed for a boat."

"He and Cairo were talking such a trip," the boy said, absently. Then more forcefully: "But the woman…the O'Shaughnessy dame…said the Russian, this Kemidov bastard, was somewhere in Frisco, and likely had the damn thing in his possession."

"What else did she tell you that night?"

The boy shook his head. "Nothing. The cops showed and I popped Gutman and got out by the fire escape." Wilmer Cook frowned. "Listen, I'll ask the questions!"

"It's your show," Spade said and shrugged again, casually. "Now you know almost as much as I do."

"What else do you know?"

The detective displayed his wolfish grin and when he whispered, it was barely audible. "I know the kind of money this dingus'll bring would set you up for life in some distant foreign land. You'd look swell in a sombrero, kid. Or maybe a turban."

Something approaching lively interest climbed into the long-lashed hazel eyes. "You're saying you'd cut me in?"

Spade cocked his head. "There's plenty of scratch to go around once we get this thing in front of the right buyer. And I got a lead on that, too. Maybe we should play on the same team this time."

The boy thought about that. Then his face wadded up like a crushed tissue, before turning a slow raging red as wheels turned in his head. "Same team! You got the damn nerve to say that to me. You who sold me out to my boss and tried to make me take the fall!"

Spade gave the boy half a smile. "Why shouldn't I? All's fair in love and war, and this is commerce, which is what makes both of those other two tick. Anyway, that's yesterday's news. What say, Wilmer?"

"I say…" And he completed the sentence with two short words, a guttural verb and "you."

"Don't be dumb, kid," Spade said, and he wasn't grinning.

Footsteps announced themselves by echoes from one direction, then more resonating footsteps from another.

"Put a lid on it, Spade," Wilmer Cook said, his whisper harsh, and backed away, resuming his position perhaps five feet from the captive.

Freddie and Eddie were on the outskirts of where the circle of light fell from above, also heading back to the position they'd previously held. Wilmer Cook turned to them, about to issue orders apparently, as Spade threw himself in his chair backward with all the force he could muster and the spindly thing broke into pieces. His broad-shouldered form rose with the clothesline bonds hanging loose, shards of wood dangling here and there from their roping like jagged teeth. Somewhat awkwardly but swiftly, Spade clawed from the narrow white ropes as if out of a clumsy cocoon, stepping free even as his captors stepped back in wide-eyed dread. Spade reached down with his right hand and selected at random a broken-off spindle and threw it like a knife at the tall clownish boy in the white-buttoned black topcoat holding the big revolver that was coming up in his right hand.

But the spindle hit the clownish figure flat in the face, startling the lad, who dropped his revolver with a resounding clunk on the concrete. Spade took this in but was already rushing the Leprechaun-faced boy brandishing the iron pipe, who was backpedaling in fear. The detective laid a thick fist in the middle of the childish face and left behind a flat runny smear of red where a nose had been and a bloody mouth that was coughing teeth.

Wilmer Cook was backing up into the dark, pulling off the glove on his right hand with his gloved left hand, apparently hoping to free his paws up to dig into his coat pocket for the automatic pistols. By this time Spade was on top of the kid with the pipe, who raised it to deliver a blow but got interrupted when the detective elbowed him in the throat. The kid went down on his knees in a prayerful mode and gurgled while Spade with his right hand snatched the iron pipe from fingers gone loose and whapped the boy alongside the head, sending him from the praying position to a general sprawl on the concrete.

The footsteps of the fleeing clown in the black white-buttoned coat echoed away in the dark accompanied by sobbing until that darkness swallowed him entirely. Spade turned to Wilmer Cook, whose gloves were off now but whose guns remained in his topcoat pockets, and with a swipe of the iron pipe caught the boy alongside his right cheek, turning it from rosy to bloody red, tearing skin. Spade clouted him again, on the same side of the head, and Wilmer Cook collapsed in a thudding pile onto the hard cold floor.

The sprawled kid, who had lost his iron pipe to the detective, was on his hands and knees crawling into the dark. Spade went over and kicked him in the seat of his pants and sent him sprawling again. But the darkness quickly consumed the boy, whose footsteps built into echoey running and then a door opening and closing, making its own echo, announced his departure. Spade felt confident the clownish one was on his buddy's heels, based upon overlapping incoherent speech from both of them far away in the darkness.

Spade walked past the fallen, moaning, barely conscious Wilmer Cook and selected a fresh if well-worn spindle-back chair from the pile of them to one side of where he'd been seated under that conical light. He sat on it, keeping an eye on the late Gutman's gunsel, and—still in his topcoat—reached under it to his suitcoat and found the sack of Bull Durham and his cigarette papers, both of which he withdrew and methodically rolled a smoke. He licked the tobacco-stuffed cylinder shut, got out his lighter and fired up the roll-your-own, then just sat enjoying it, his breath heavy from the minor exertion of taking these children to the woodshed, which only made the taking in of the tobacco that much more pleasurable.

Finally Spade rose, put his cigarette out under his right heel, and went over and dragged Wilmer Cook to the unbroken spindle chair, then sat him bodily in it. All around, like the confetti aftermath of a parade, were the broken pieces of the chair Spade had risen from and the clothesline he had shed. He helped himself to the big automatic pistols in either of the boy's topcoat pockets and, careful not to pitch them hard and risk them firing, tossed the iron weapons sliding into the void.

Spade fetched himself another chair, kicked away the refuse of the broken one including loose clothesline, and sat facing Wilmer Cook, waiting for the slumped boy to come around.

After a while, Spade said, "Now you're just faking it. No

strategizing is going to get you out of this. But cooperate and you may live to see morning."

The hazel eyes came slowly open.

"…You got the best of me," Wilmer Cook whimpered. "What else is there to it?"

"There's who sent you."

The boy's lower lip trembled. "Nobody sent me. I'm on my own."

"You've never been on your own in your entire tiny little life," Spade said contemptuously. "Your mother or your grandma or your aunt or whoever raised you most likely was still dressing you till you got up and left for the big city."

The long lashes fluttered and tears like dew hung there. "Go ahead. Kill me. See if I care."

Spade shook his head. "Who are you trying to protect? This little shindig tonight, you probably organized that yourself. Bully for you, son. Your boss said, Go get some boys and grab Sam Spade. Whoever the boss is, he'd know you wouldn't be up to it on your own. But he didn't guess you'd go to the school-yard for your backup."

Wilmer Cook spoke his two favorite words.

Spade slapped him. It rang in the high-ceilinged chamber. The boy began to cry. Not weeping or sobbing, just emitting a trickle of tears on a face no longer rosy-cheeked but dirt-smudged from his fall.

Spade's voice was flat, detached. "Who sent you, son? I won't embarrass you this time. I don't mind slapping you around but it's a waste of my time and yours. Because you're going to tell me."

"Dixie Monahan," Wilmer Cook said, like a little kid admitting he stole a pie.

"Dixie Monahan the gambler," Spade said. "The Chicago gambler."

The boy nodded.

"Why?" Spade asked.

"Why do you think?" Wilmer Cook said, with pitiful defiance. "Find out what you know about the falcon. If the thing's really in town. If you know who has it. Or if you got it yourself, somewhere. Why do you think?"

Spade mulled what he'd heard, then said, "All right. I'll buy it. Where's Monahan staying?"

"The Belvedere."

"Under his own name?"

"No. Monty Dixon."

"What room number?"

"Dunno. We met in the hotel bar."

"…Okay, then." Spade pushed the chair back, rose, said: "I see you or any of your friends again, none of you will walk away from it. Understood?"

Wilmer Cook nodded.

Spade wagged a finger at him. "Sit here and think about the bad things you've done," he said sarcastically, "and when I've been gone a while, five minutes say? Get up and get out and hop that freight like I advised."

Spade turned and the boy dove for him.

Having anticipated such a move, Spade turned back and grabbed the boy by the topcoat and flung him against a wall of tables, which groaned but maintained its stacked structure.

"Something you should know about me," Spade said. "I always pay back my debts."

Still on the floor, the boy managed, "…what?"

"Remember how you said goodbye to me, after your boss fed me the knock-out drops?"

Wilmer Cook frowned.

The detective went over and drew his right foot back and

kicked Wilmer Cook in the temple. The kick rolled the boy over on his side, where he passed out. Whether the sleeping gunsel would still be on the cement floor when workers arrived was a problem Wilmer Cook would have to deal with himself.

As for Spade, he was smiling to himself, pleased to have the books settled.

CHAPTER SIX
The Honeymoon Suite

Boyish but pretty in a thin pale blue cotton dress, Effie Perine—sitting with folded hands at the edge of the client's chair opposite Spade behind his desk—took in her employer's tale of thwarted youthful kidnappers and bold escape and general derring-do as if engulfed by an episode in a moving picture serial.

Spade, offhandedly delivering his account, seemed more interested in creating his latest hand-rolled cigarette than imparting any sense of danger. He left out certain unflattering pieces of it—kicking Wilmer Cook in the head, for example—but after he'd completed his casual account, the lighting of that cigarette lent shadows and strange color to his somewhat satanic features.

"Look, precious," he said, nothing dreamy about the yellow-grey eyes now, "I mention all this blood-and-thunder stuff only to alert you. This damned Maltese falcon affair has kicked up again and I don't know how rough it might get. So be watchful."

"Do you want me to get one of those…things from the safe?" she asked, her brown eyes so big they showed white all around.

"We don't have to be ridiculous about it," he said.

"I don't think when you're being assaulted on a city street," she said defensively, "you should hesitate to carry a weapon."

"I hate the damn things," Spade said, meaning handguns. "They cause more trouble than they're worth."

She lifted her shoulders in a shrug that took a while to come down. "There's a little snubby one I could carry in my purse. If you're worried about my health."

The cigarette hung from his lower lip; his eyes were hooded. "Do you know how to use it?"

"You took me to that firing range last year. Or was it two years ago?"

"Damnit," he said to himself. He sighed smoke. "Go ahead. Pack your shooting iron, Annie Oakley. Just don't go blasting away at every potential target."

That got a little smile out of her. She retrieved her notebook, which she had set on his desk but hadn't used on this trip, rose and flounced off. He watched her with a smile that quickly darkened.

She paused at the door between Spade's office and hers. "Maybe you should 'pack' one yourself."

He shook his head. "No room in my purse."

She laughed at that. But just a little, then returned to her world and shut him in his.

The muggy day requiring no topcoat, the brim of his dark grey fedora tugged down, Spade prowled the Belvedere lobby with its pale green walls, plush red Oriental carpets and swooping white marble staircase, in search of a certain hotel detective.

He found the round-faced middle-aged dick leaning against the counter at the cigar-stand, flirting with a clerk half his age, a brunette girl who was just enough past plain that a hotel detective might make a suitable sugar daddy.

Seeing Spade approach, Ralph Lucas, "Luke" to one and all, moved away from his objective. The two detectives muttered "Morning" to each other and discreetly shook hands, Spade leaving a fin behind. Luke's face was white and his suit was black, his dark eyes shrewd.

"What can I do for you, Sam?" Luke said, slipping the bill away into a jingling pants pocket.

They spoke in quiet tones, not quite whispers. Nearby, overstuffed men in overstuffed chairs were enjoying their White Owls and Havanas, reading their morning *Calls*, pausing to take in women walking by. Cigar smoke floated, clouds that would never make rain.

Spade said: "You have a guest named Dixon. Monty Dixon or possibly Montgomery. I could use a room number. And whether he's in or not."

The hotel dick nodded. "Give me a minute."

Luke went to the front desk and returned in less time than that.

"Yeah, he's in," Luke said. "His real name's Dixie Monahan, by the way. If Dixie is anybody's real name."

"You know this guest?"

"He's the kind you make sure you know. He has the look. Black suit with white pinstripes, diamond stickpin. Mob type or big-time gambler maybe. Here's the good part."

"Oh?" Spade began making himself a cigarette, taking his time, expertly pouring Bull Durham flakes into the fold of paper.

Luke was good at sideways smiles and gave Spade one. "Our guest slips me a double sawbuck and says to call if anybody comes asking for him. Dressed like that, he thinks he's under wraps? Jesus. All he lacked was a neon sign. Takes all kinds, I guess."

"So I hear." Spade licked the cigarette paper's edge. "You going to call him on the house phone after I get on the elevator?"

The palm that came up might have been a traffic cop's. "That five's a binding transaction, Sam. Anyway, you and me, we go way back."

"Yeah," Spade said with a grin. "All the way to the last time I slipped you a fin. Did this one buy me a room number?"

The palm waved Spade's question away. "Sure. Eight-oh-seven."

"Isn't that the Honeymoon suite?"

Luke's sideways smile came back out. "You got a good memory, Sammy."

One of Spade's V-shaped eyebrows flattened out above a widened yellow-grey eye. "He have anybody in there with him? A female maybe?"

"He might. He's been here a week and usually does."

"Anybody I know?"

His mouth laughed but nothing came out; hotel dicks didn't like attracting attention. "Different one every night. Some you might know, hell, maybe all of 'em. Sally Stanford sends them over."

Stanford was the most notorious if reliable madam in San Francisco.

Spade was lighting up his cigarette. "Thanks, Luke."

Luke tilted his head, narrowed an eye. "He does have company, I understand."

"Oh?"

"Bruiser of a bodyguard. Best be on your toes, boyo."

Spade's cigarette went cockily up, the tip just missing his nose. "Like a ballet dancer."

Luke nodded, then mustered a sympathetic frown. "Say, how was Miles' funeral?"

Spade snapped his lighter shut, put it away. "Not much of a turnout."

"Sorry I couldn't make it. They work me like a dog in this place."

"I noticed," Spade said, with a glance at the cigar-stand girl. "Mostly it was relatives paid their respects. I remembered you to the widow."

Luke grinned. "I bet you did."

After another quick handshake, one that didn't leave any money behind, Spade let Luke return to the not quite plain clerk.

Spade rode up to the eighth floor, emerged and disposed of his cigarette in a wall ashtray between two elevators, then strode to 807, where he knocked. It took two tries before he got an answer.

The answer was a big man with the kind of dark jowls that shaving couldn't do much about and bushy eyebrows that only made the lamb-dropping orbs beneath seem smaller. A mashed nose and cauliflower ears spoke of a prize-fighting career that hadn't necessarily gone well and the unbuttoned ready-made suit was a dark blue, with an indifferently knotted flap of a tie alternating pale stripes with two shades of blue, a little wider than was in style. The butt of a revolver poked up from his belt and dimpled his shirt.

"Samuel Spade to see Mr. Dixon."

The responding voice was a breathy rasp too high to fit the ex-boxer's general appearance. "You ain't got a appointment."

"I'm aware I ain't got a appointment. Please tell Mr. Dixon I'd like a few moments of his time about the Maltese falcon."

"About the falckin' what?"

"Just tell him. He'll want to know."

The ex-boxer thought about that, grunted and closed the door on Spade. Muffled conversation could be heard through the heavy barrier. The ex-boxer returned and opened the door, standing aside for the visitor.

The sitting room of the suite, with its eggshell-white walls, was all whites and greys and blacks and *art moderne* furnishings, although of the rounded, padded variety, not the sculpted wood kind. On a central couch, in an area carpeted in geometric shapes of grey-white-and-black, lounged a man of forty or so in white-pinstriped black trousers above which was the top red half of a long-sleeved union suit. Spade's unenthusiastic host was lowering the pulp publication—*Detective Story Magazine*—that he'd been reading to view his unexpected guest.

Presumably Monty Dixon or Dixie Monahan, a rose by any name, the man on the light-grey rounded couch had his bare feet up on a matching divan. He was handsome in a Douglas Fairbanks, skimpily mustached manner but a bit battered, as if one or two of Doug's stunts had gone awry.

"He'll have to stand for a frisk," the man on the couch said, still peering over the pulp.

That mellow baritone contrasted with the bodyguard's high-pitched rasp to Spade: "You gotta stand for a frisk," as if he were interpreting.

Spade said, "Sure," and raised his hands.

The ex-boxer patted him down, but when the bodyguard's thick palm seemed headed for Spade's groin, the detective said, "Frisk is fine. Frisky isn't. That's all you get."

The ex-boxer looked confused, as if he'd never been challenged before, though his cauliflower ears and mashed nose indicated otherwise. The brutish guardian at the gate froze, hands mid-air, mulling this conundrum, when Spade yanked the .38 Colt New Service revolver from the ex-boxer's waistband, pointed it at him and eased past him, backing up. Spade moved to the couch, where he took the seat next to his amused mustached host, then set the weapon on the end table nearby.

"I guess," the probable Dixie Monahan said, "you are Samuel Spade."

"Call me Sam."

"Call me Dix."

"Dix it is."

Dixie Monahan said to the ex-boxer, standing there like a stuffed polar bear in a museum, "K.O., Mr. Spade and I are going to talk business."

"Yessir," K.O. said, not liking it, and sullenly grabbed a straight-back chair near the door and went out into the hall dragging it and shut himself out.

Spade said: "Is that what we're going to talk? Business?"

Dixie Monahan flipped a hand. "I'll follow your lead. You called this meeting, Sam."

Spade folded his arms. "Actually, you called it, Dix. When you sent Wilmer Cook and his playmates to roust me."

The gambler's smile was perfect and white and slightly oversized, the best money could buy. "I'm not up on the local talent. Apparently I picked poorly."

Spade's reluctant host reached for a humidor on the end table on his side of the futuristic couch and fingered out a small dark cigar. He produced a lighter from a pants pocket and fired the little dark tube, then puffed it to life. "Care for a cigarillo, Sam? I'm partial to these *Partagás*."

"No thanks."

Hearing something behind him, Spade glanced back. A sleepy young woman of perhaps twenty-five had exited a bedroom door. She wore a short pink chemise that revealed long shapely legs and barely covered a pert bottom, hair a Louise Brooks bob, eyes big and dark brown and almost as prettily long-lashed as Wilmer Cook's. The bee-stung lips bore no lipstick and didn't need any.

She paused just behind and between the seated Spade and Dixie Monahan and said to the latter, in a tired baby-doll voice, "Want some coffee, Mr. Dixon? I'll get some going."

"That'd be swell, kid," Monahan said. He looked at Spade. "How about you, Sam?"

"Sure. Black."

Her expression blankly pretty, the girl looked at Spade as if she'd just noticed his presence, which was perhaps the case.

Dixie Monahan said, "Some cream in mine, sweetie."

She nodded and went off through a door to the rear right.

"There's a kitchenette," Spade's host informed him, as if that was the remarkable thing about the girl's entry and offer.

"All the comforts of home," Spade said.

The mustached man's big white teeth filled out an endless smile. "Now, Sam, I hope we can put this little matter behind us."

"What matter would that be?"

The gambler offered up a fleeting, unconvincing grimace. "Wilmer Cook's uncalled-for clumsy approach."

"That's one way to describe getting tied into a chair and beaten."

Dixie Monahan let out a mouthful of smoke. "Meaning no offense, you look none the worse for wear. And when Mr. Cook dropped by late last night for his payment, he looked like hell. When I heard his story, little of which I bought, I docked him half his rate and kicked him out."

"Who was it said a good man is hard to find?" Spade leaned forward slightly, smiling with tight lips. "Perhaps I might tie *you* in a chair and work you over. And if you think that plug-ugly sitting out in the hallway could stop me, you're not as smart as you look."

The gambler laughed out cigarillo smoke. "You disappoint me, Sam. That kind of tough talk is more typical of the Wilmer Cooks of the world than a man of your reputation."

Spade's smile turned mild, his yellow-grey eyes dreamy. "I was just trying to tune in on the wavelength of somebody who reads detective pulps."

The gambler gestured vaguely with a left hand whose fourth finger bore a fat diamond in a fancy silver setting. "Let's not get off on the wrong foot, Sam. Would it help if I apologized for last night's clumsy effort?"

"Sure." Spade's smile turned into a nasty grin with some teeth in it. "That and a cup of coffee from that cutie in the kitchenette'll go a long goddamn way with me."

With half-lidded eyes, Dixie Monahan studied his guest. "Perhaps information would go even further than a cup of coffee in this instance."

"I'm listening," Spade said.

"What do you know about Floyd Thursby?"

Spade's words came as casual as their content was not. "I know he's dead. Shot and killed. I know the O'Shaughnessy dame did it. He and Miles Archer…my late partner? Were acquainted somehow, maybe in business. Met in Chicago on some matter or another. When the O'Shaughnessy twist came to me with a trumped-up story about an apparently non-existent sister, and Miles heard Floyd Thursby's name being part it, he held back from me."

"Disappointing."

Spade's tight smile returned. "He was a shifty bastard. Don't waste any tears on him. I didn't."

Dixie Monahan put on amused shock. "No sympathy for your late partner?"

"Just self-recrimination for going in business with him in the first place. You'd think a guy in my line would be a better judge of character. But then there's a chance you know more about his dealings with Thursby than I do."

"Floyd and Archer knew each other," the gambler affirmed, "and had some dealings before Thursby came to work for me. As a bodyguard."

Spade gestured with a thumb at the door. "Was Thursby of the same stripe as that mug in the hall?"

The gambler shook his head. "Floyd Thursby was a killer. As

hard, as tough a man as you'll meet, and I would imagine you've met a few."

"A few."

Dixie Monahan looked to one side of Spade as if the past might be back there. "Thursby worked as an enforcer for a South Side Chicago mob. When the top boys wanted somebody roughed up, he was their favorite strongarm. When they wanted somebody to talk, he was their on-call convincer. When they wanted somebody gone, he pulled off a disappearing act that would make Houdini go green. But he had a weakness."

The Louise Brooks babydoll came out of the kitchen with two cups on saucers balanced in either delicate, red-nailed hand. She floated over, delivered a tan-surfaced cup to Dixie Monahan and a black-shimmering-topped one to Spade. She winked at the private eye, with her back to the other man, though her expression otherwise remained as blank as a bisque baby's.

After she'd gone back for another cup for herself in the kitchenette, and returned to head toward the open bedroom door, Spade said, stopping her, "Trade you."

Her frown of confusion didn't stop her from swapping coffee cups with Spade. They were both drinking it black, after all.

"Test it for me," Spade said to her. "See if it's too hot or maybe not hot enough."

She sipped what had been Spade's coffee. "It's just right," she said.

"Thanks, baby bear," he said. "Have another sip."

She did.

"Now go over by the bedroom door," the detective said. "Just till you finish that cup."

The girl glanced at Dixie Monahan, who gave her a vaguely irritated nod to do so. She did, sitting on an ivory-colored straight back chair and drinking delicately from the cup, knees primly together.

Spade said to the gambler, "Like you, Floyd Thursby liked the dolls. Is that the weakness you made reference to?"

Dixie Monahan grunted humorlessly. "Apparently your partner, Miles Archer, had a similar soft spot."

"Frails *are* a common male frailty, all right." Spade set his coffee cup on the end table. The chemise-sporting girl with the Louise Brooks bob kept sipping her black coffee, apparently oblivious to the two men's conversation.

Spade continued: "You want to get on my good side, Dix? Fill in the missing pieces. The D.A. was interested in fitting you up for the Archer and Thursby murders, and concocted a tale where Thursby got himself killed by Chicago mob boys over you welshing on a bet. It sounded like nonsense to me at the time, and now the D.A. is just fine with hanging the O'Shaughnessy broad for Archer, and the cops are looking for your boy Cook to take the fall for Thursby."

"Wilmer Cook is not my boy," the gambler said, irritatedly, after a sip of his creamy coffee. "I told you I don't know the local talent. *He* came to *me*."

"Came to you?"

Dixie Monahan nodded. "The boy said he could make you talk."

That got a laugh out of Spade, a harsh one. "That damn kid? About what, for Christ's sake?"

The gambler had another sip, then said slyly, "About what else, Sam? The falcon. The Maltese falcon."

The crease between Spade's eyebrows deepened. "How does a Chicago gambler know a goddamn thing about that lousy damn bird?"

The response was a throwaway gesture. "A gambler stays on

top of the game by gathering information. You know that, Sam. What you don't know is why somebody in my position would go on the hunt for some medieval artifact."

"You do have me there." Spade turned to the girl in the ivory chair. "Are you finished with that cup, honey?"

"Yes." Confused though she was, that's all she had to say about it.

"Good. Go back in the bedroom and shut the door behind you, would you?"

She nodded and followed their guest's orders, taking the empty cup along.

"What was that about?" Dixie Monahan, looking like an aggravated half-dressed devil in his red union suit shirt. He and V-featured Spade made quite the satanic pair.

"Somebody fed me knock-out drops in a drink a week or so ago," Spade said affably. "I thought maybe coffee would work just as well."

"Christ. If you don't trust me, just say so."

"I don't trust you."

The gambler shook his head. "Let's see if I can build some.... Have you spent much time in Chicago?"

"None."

The flummoxed host took a deep breath, free of cigar smoke, and began: "Somehow I got myself tied in with the Chicago crowd. Long story, not pertinent. But I wound up running a roadhouse for them. One of the most profitable casino nightclubs outside of the city. Around then I had a bad run of cards and wound up owing some money to friends of my new business associates, and I, uh, helped myself to some of the proceeds from the casino to pay 'em off...figuring I could catch up soon enough."

"And you didn't."

His shrug admitted it. "I didn't. I knew Thursby from high-stakes games in St. Louis and, before I left the States, hired him on as my bodyguard. He was somebody few of those Chicago boys wanted to mess with—he'd kill a man over an insult. Without blinking. He seemed to be just what I needed. At any rate, I was working the casinos in Hong Kong when Thursby got himself caught up with this O'Shaughnessy woman. Floyd came back to me abuzz with a story about a golden, jeweled falcon that was supposedly worth a million or more. At the same time, he was obviously goofy as a damn kid over this broad. The idea was he'd get in with this fat man Gutman and his crew, a team of grifters who'd been running con games on several continents—that Joel Cairo character was part of it, and Wilmer Cook and Gutman's daughter Rhea, and O'Shaughnessy of course. Gutman had been after this golden jeweled statuette for years and years, it seems, and somehow got wind it was in this deposed Russian general's possession."

"Kemidov," Spade said.

"Kemidov. Who supposedly didn't know the value of what he had. The idea was the broad would seduce the Russian, worm her way into his world, and Thursby would steal the statue, killing the general if need be. He was a ruthless son of a bitch, Thursby, would rub a guy out like a mean kid stepping on an ant hill."

"I'm getting that impression," Spade said.

"My job was to line up a buyer," the gambler said, "and I had plenty of connections. I ran games with some of the richest men in America in my day."

"Before you went in with Chicago."

The gambler raised his eyebrows and set them back down. "Not the smartest move, but I was busted and my rep as a well-known high-roller was the only card I had left to play at the time. Which is how I wound up running a roadhouse for the Chicago boys."

"We went over that already," Spade said, annoyed. "Get back to Thursby and O'Shaughnessy."

Dixie Monahan's coffee cup was empty but he still was smoking the cigarillo, which trailed grey in his gesturing hand. "Well, the loving couple ditched me. Took off for the States without me. The dame shipped the statue out somehow, and she and Thursby took a fast boat home. Must've had a buyer in their pocket or anyway came up with one.... That's everything I know, Sam."

"Not everything," Spade said, and something nasty came into his smile. "You sicced Wilmer Cook on me, didn't you? Why?"

A swearing-in-court palm came up. "I still have Chicago breathing down my damn neck! If I can lay hands on that falcon, I can pay off my debtors and still have one hell of a stake left to make my comeback. Hell, maybe I'll retire! Supposedly the Russian has the falcon. Can you confirm that?"

Spade shook his head. "I can confirm only that I have a client interested in me finding the thing. A client willing to share in whatever price it may bring."

The gambler was studying him like a tricky hand of cards. "How married are you to this client?"

Spade shrugged. "Not married at all. A happy bachelor."

Thrusting his forefinger at the private eye, Dixie Monahan made his bid: "I will give you a thousand-dollar retainer and a quarter of what I realize on the artifact."

"A gee to find the falcon?"

"A gee to find the falcon. With the possibility, the promise, of much more."

Spade glanced around the *art moderne* sitting room. "You know, for a guy who's broke and owes Chicago untold thousands, you seem to be pretty flush. I mean, girls from Sally Stanford's don't come cheap. Now you're throwing a grand around. Is it real or just talk?"

The gambler shook a fist like he was about to throw dice. "Sam, my oversized debt to Chicago aside, I never said I was broke. I've been operating games out of this hotel room for two weeks now, and trust me—San Francisco has no shortage of suckers."

"Just so you don't think I'm one of them," Spade said. "I'll take that thousand now."

CHAPTER SEVEN
The Retainer

The sun had long since set and the moon was high by the time Spade returned to his office. He had asked Effie Perine to wait till he got back so he could stay on top of any calls that might come in. He found her not at her desk but at his, sleeping on her elbowed arms winged like a school kid napping, but with a little .380 Remington pistol looking big in her delicate hand. A new touch of some white lights draped the modest Christmas tree but the inner office was otherwise dark.

Spade sat in the client's chair, which scraped enough as he backed it into place for her to wake and sit up, startled, and point the pistol at him.

"If you aren't the cutest thing I ever saw," Spade said with a mocking V of a smile, getting his tobacco pouch and rolling papers out of his suitcoat pocket.

The brown-eyed girl put the weapon down. She had a nicely mussed look as she pouted at him.

"I was getting worried," she said.

"Not worried enough to stay awake," he said lightly, as he made his cigarette, cross-legged, leaning back in the chair.

"It must be the middle of the night," she said with a pretty frown and stretching her arms as she yawned. She switched on the desk lamp and threw brightness on half of them, the rest still in the dark.

"It's just a little after seven," Spade said, lighting up. "Let's go get something to eat."

She made a face. "I'll need to call my mother."

Spade pointed. "The phone's right there."

Effie Perine said little for a while and maintained a sullen posture on the cab ride to Telegraph Hill and the restaurant Spade chose, Julius' Castle, a venue shaped as its name suggested though its pink-painted exterior lent it a whimsical touch. The interior of the place invoked a Victorian-era parlor style, formal and cozy at once, and not terribly busy tonight.

They sat at a secluded table-for-two by a window against a backdrop of ferryboats crossing this way and that while city lights winked across the bay, as if somebody knew something they didn't. This castle was in part a speakeasy, which allowed Spade to partake of a Manhattan and his companion a glass of wine as they waited for dinner to arrive.

"The Richmond district," Spade said, referring to the enclave of Russian-speaking immigrants along Geary Boulevard, "didn't give me a damn thing toward locating this General Kemidov."

"You tried the Russian Tea Room, of course," Effie Perine said, past her pouting stage now.

"I did. Two of the four owners were there."

Spade's wide-eyed secretary said, "They're all former members of the Russian Imperial Ballet, you know."

"So they say. Both shared one thing in common."

"Oh?"

"If General Kemidov came into their establishment, they'd poison his food."

"Oh."

Spade ordered the Julius Veal and Effie Perine the Specialty Broiled Chicken. Orchestral music on the radio filtered in, punctuated by the occasional foghorn. Over Cherries Jubilee, Spade picked up the conversation.

"Kemidov is one of these Imperial Russian Army guys who fled from the Bolsheviks," the detective said, spooning cherries and ice cream. "He'd been no friend in the Mother Land to the upper-class types who lost everything, or artists and intellectuals, either. Seems like Kemidov's somebody with plenty of enemies from back home. That's why he settled in the Orient."

"And now he's in San Francisco," Spade's secretary said.

"Would seem so," Spade admitted. "But he sure as hell hasn't taken up residence in the Richmond district with the other Russians. There's a little colony of 'em on Potrero Hill I can try, and another bunch west of Fillmore and south of Sutter. I better work myself up a real appetite for vodka and caviar."

"A good private detective," Effie Perine said, "could probably find a stray Russian general in San Francisco."

"Go ahead," he said with a half a smile. "Needle me, my little addle-brained angel. See what it gets you."

She shrugged. "It got me broiled chicken, didn't it?"

They were in another cab when Spade said, "I forgot to ask —any calls?"

"Nothing notable but your client, Rhea Gutman. She'd like a report. She's at the Alexandria. Room 12-C."

"Her late father's room," Spade said.

"Apparently he never checked out," Effie Perine said.

"Oh, he checked out, all right."

Spade had the cab take her to her mother's house on Ninth Avenue.

The following morning Spade walked the four blocks from his office building to the Alexandria, a twenty-two-story luxury hotel freshly opened that October. He strolled through an English Renaissance lobby too lavishly appointed for comfort, where massive murals of Sir Francis Drake's arrival in what would be California loomed in a reminder of conquest. He checked at the desk to see if Miss Gutman was in and was told she was.

"Should I call upstairs and announce you, sir?"

"Don't bother. I'm expected."

Spade took an elevator up to the twelfth floor and at 12-C knocked once, waited, knocked again, and was poised to try one last time when his client Rhea Gutman answered in a glistening neck-to-ankle yellow dressing gown that indicated it had been put hurriedly on over damp naked flesh. The effect was of being completely covered and yet wearing nothing at all.

He had seen this gown before, when the girl's loopy condition had him helping her walk off the drug-induced ruse her father had staged to give himself and his retinue time to search Spade's apartment and office for the prize falcon. But that was last week, and this week the dampness under the garment created a whole new effect.

The girl clutched the collar of her dressing gown as if embarrassed, despite just having knowingly answered the door in such a figure-revealing state. Her heart-shaped face, with its big golden-brown eyes bereft of make-up, seemed almost ghostly in its paleness and utter youth.

"Oh, Mr. Spade," Rhea Gutman said, the sleek arcs of fair hair that he'd seen her in before transformed now into a nest of darker, water-pearled curls. "I wasn't expecting you."

She opened the door a wide crack and he stepped into the pale green-walled suite with its windows onto the street and three closed doors to separate bedrooms—her own one of them, the others formerly her father's and possibly Joel Cairo's or Wilmer Cook's, or some combination of those ambiguously entwined men.

"I told them at the desk," Spade lied, "to call and alert you."

"I was just showering," she said, an explanation of the obvious. "If you'll excuse me…"

"Sure."

She went into the bedroom at far left.

It was here, in this rather large sitting room with its money-green carpet and rounded olive furnishings, that Spade had first encountered Casper Gutman; had heard the history of the Maltese falcon; had been served by the girl's father a Mickey Finn; and had been kicked in the head by Wilmer Cook. Here, too, Rhea Gutman had played at being heavily drugged for him to help her walk it off. None of this showed on Spade's features as he tossed his hat on a table by the door.

Moving toward the middle of the room, he paused and waited until the girl in the damp dressing gown emerged, her wet hair now towel-turbaned like a native from somewhere.

"My secretary said you'd like a report," Spade said, matter of fact. "I'm afraid little if any of it will please you much."

"Can I get you something to drink?" she offered, and motioned to a liquor cart.

"It's a little early." Then he thought about it. "A touch of rum-and-Coca-Cola wouldn't hurt. If you have ice, that too please."

Rhea Gutman went over and made that for him as he settled onto a lime-green couch. As she was dropping two ice cubes in, with her back to him, Spade's eyes were on the mystery of a figure that could be that slim and yet so shapely.

His hostess returned with two glasses, hefting hers and saying with a little smile, "Orange juice," then handed him a snifter of dark liquid that was significantly more than a touch. He took it, sipped it. Any hesitancy due to the doctored drink her father had slipped him last week was not apparent in the dreamy calmness of his face.

She sat next to him, leaving most of a cushion between, and placed her glass of orange juice on a coaster on the coffee table squatting in front of them. Her hands settled on her knees, a rather prim posture for a girl whose nakedness was a thin skin of cloth away.

"What have you learned?" she asked. "Have you located this General Kemidov?"

"I have not," Spade told her, and informed her of his efforts in the Richmond district and touched on what he had left to do today and possibly thereafter in other Russian areas of the city.

"It certainly does sound as if," Rhea Gutman said, "a person in your line of work has to perform all sorts of tedious tasks. You certainly earn your pay."

"It does come with the territory," he said. "Pounding the pavement, some call it. Shoe leather." He sipped his rum-and-Coca-Cola. "Reminds me of a job that came in once, from a Seattle agency."

"It does?"

Spade nodded, leaning back, swirling the dark liquid in its glass. "One of my first assignments, over a decade ago. I was working for the local branch of the Continental Detective Agency—they're second only to Pinkerton's, you know. Anyway, they assigned me to find a young man named Collinson who had hired on with their Seattle branch with, it turned out, research in mind…to pursue dreams of being a heroic detective in the Sherlock Holmes manner. The lad did some actual sleuthing for Continental, but ultimately got assigned to be a strike-breaker for mining interests in Wyoming. Rumor has it he was offered $3,000 to be part of killing a certain labor leader, but turned it down. After that labor leader was beaten to death by six unidentified strike-breakers, Collinson was questioned but released, then disappeared. The law wasn't looking for him, but his banker father was, hoping to drag his boy back into the business world. Took months, but I tracked Collinson to New York where he'd been for a time, writing about detective heroes for the dime novels, Nick Carter and so on. He'd used a pen name to which he soon changed his name legally, and that was part of why it took a while to locate him. His vivid writing attracted attention and he'd been wooed across country to Hollywood to become a screenwriter, his credits including numerous mystery yarns. He was paid $3,000 a week. Which is the part that made sense to me out of what happened after that. I tracked him back to California, Los Angeles of course, but I was too late to be of any real help. It became my distasteful duty to inform the banker father that the boy had committed suicide. Went out a high window. I never told the father what the note his son had left had said."

She'd been listening intently, taking an occasional orange-juice sip. "What did it say?"

" 'I was one of the six.' "

"...How terribly sad," Rhea Gutman said, though her eyes were clear and unclouded. "I don't suppose you think you'll find this Russian general has committed suicide."

"No!" Spade said, and laughed. "No Dutch Act for the good general. Particularly not if he's holding the Maltese falcon and the promise of untold millions. Or maybe hundreds of thousands, or even just thousands, since exaggeration seems to be built into this thing. But even one thousand can get people killed."

Rhea Gutman scooted a bit closer to her guest, both hands hugging the glass of orange juice. She frowned a little. "Are you implying my retainer for your services wasn't...sufficient?"

"Let's not get ahead of ourselves," Spade said. He had some of his rum-and-Coca-Cola. "There's more to report."

He proceeded to tell her the rest of it—how he'd met with both Joel Cairo and Brigid O'Shaughnessy at County Jail #1; how Cairo had a wealthy buyer in his pocket and would provide the name if the Levantine were brought in for a share of what the falcon realized; how Brigid O'Shaughnessy had somewhat surprisingly encouraged him to help Rhea Gutman, confirming that the girl's father had misused Rhea and made a Judas sheep out of her; how professional gambler Dixie Monahan offered Spade a thousand dollars if the falcon could be found; and finally, ignoring chronology, how Wilmer Cook and two cronies had grabbed Spade and grilled and beaten him before he turned the tables on them.

Though Spade's recounting of the screenwriter who committed suicide had not extracted tears from the girl, the assault on the private detective by Wilmer Cook and his cronies appeared to upset Rhea Gutman a good deal. She covered her mouth and lurched into his arms and embraced him.

"Oh, Mr. Spade," she said through sobs, "what I've put you through…I'm so very sorry. I had no idea what sort of danger I was subjecting you to…what I was thoughtlessly putting you through!"

"Well, your father's killing," Spade said coldly, "and the other two murders might have been a clue."

She pulled away, something in the wide eyes now— not what had happened to Spade, but his reaction to her concern.

"With what I've got left to do," Spade said, and his tone had turned clinical, "I'll be searching half of San Francisco for this Russian general among a greater concentration of White émigrés than could be found anywhere else in the United States. I don't think a grand is going to cover it."

Her finely sculpted eyebrows rose. "You…you want more?"

"We're talking about a *rara avis* that might be worth millions and has already cost three lives in a matter of days—including your own father's. I can return five C's to you and be done with it, or you can kick in another five and I stay on the job."

She could not have looked more shocked if he'd slapped her.

"You'd...you'd ask for more money from me? When you know how little I have?"

Spade's sigh came from low in his belly. He set the almost-empty rum snifter on its coaster and ice clinked. "I have no idea how little or how much you have. I'm a business not a charity, and there's only so much I'm willing to gamble on the come."

A small delicate hand found a tissue in a pocket of the dressing gown. She wept into the thing, shaking.

"The tears look real, anyway," Spade said, studying her. "And I buy the fear. Kicking in another five hundred would cinch it."

She stood quickly, gave him an indignant look, then ran to the far bedroom door, behind which she disappeared.

Spade finished his rum-and-Coca-Cola.

Rhea Gutman returned, face dry, expression sulky. The towel turban had fallen off during her bedroom excursion, exposing the tight damp curls. She walked toward Spade like a tin soldier and held out three one-hundred-dollar bills.

"This is all I have," she said.

Spade scowled. "That's everything?"

Her chin came up. "I kept a little to live on."

"How little?"

"Fifty dollars."

Spade considered that. "Okay," he said, and took the three bills. "This will have to do. I'll give it the rest of today and tomorrow."

Her eyes, red but tearless now, bored into him. "Has anyone else given you money in this?"

"Sorry, darling." His wolfish smile was brief. "The Samuel Spade Agency offers strict client confidentiality."

And he went out.

CHAPTER EIGHT
The Man in the Morgue

His union suit doubling as pajamas, Spade sat on the edge of his made bed, lowered from its wall box in his Post Street apartment, soaking his bare feet in a small tub of very warm water and Epsom Salts, a mixture he'd concocted in his small kitchen. The detective's afternoon and early evening had taken a toll on his lower extremities as he visited businesses and occasional residences in the Potrero Hill colony of Russians, and the enclave west of Fillmore.

"That leaves the nest of Russian émigrés south of Sutter for tomorrow," he'd told his secretary at the office before shooing Effie Perine home around six-thirty. He locked up and walked over to the Palace Hotel where in its restaurant he had Salisbury steak with peas and a baked potato. Then he headed to his apartment and settled into the small couch by the window for a succession of rolled cigarettes and three wine glasses of Bacardi while he read the latest *Ring* magazine. Before long, with his bed lowered and his aching feet toweled off, he was in the process of dragging back the covers to climb in under them when the telephone rang.

Standing there in his thin white union suit like his own ghost, he growled and lifted the candlestick phone's receiver, stopping the ring if not his annoyance. The alarm clock perched atop *Duke's Celebrated Cases of America* on a table near his bedside informed him it was ten minutes till midnight.

A familiar hoarse voice said: "Sam, it's Tom."

"Who's dead this time?" Spade said, only half-kidding.

"It ain't funny, Sam." Tom Polhaus' side of the call carried a noticeable echo. "I'm calling from the morgue. The Lieutenant wants you down here."

"What if I want to know why?"

Even the cop's sigh echoed. "Just come down here, Sam. You don't need to get in any worse with the Lieutenant."

"Why, is he mad at me for solving his cases?" Spade's nasty grin made it into his voice. "Tell Dundy to call me himself and make it civil this time. Maybe I'll consider his request."

"Don't be that way, Sam. He told me to call and ask polite, he really did."

"And if that didn't work?"

Tom sighed again, almost a groan this time, the echo still there. "He said he has just the judge to contact at home to get a warrant sworn out and make you a material witness."

"A material witness of what in the hell?"

"Come down to the morgue and see. You'll probably be able to make this go away soon enough."

"Probably?"

"Just get over here, Sam. Or would you really rather spend the night in a cell? You know where to find us."

"Yeah," Spade said. "I know where to find you."

For the second time this week Spade made his way to the County Jail #1 building, where the Coroner's Office and City Mortuary were located on the first two floors. He went down an unmarked alley into a U-shaped court on the east side and went in the main entrance. He checked in with the officer on the door, then the visitor's footsteps made little gunshot echoes as he crossed the marble floor to the pebbled-glass-and-wood exterior of his destination. He went in.

The whiteness of the surprisingly small, sparse office, with its single built-in floor-to-near-ceiling white cabinet, contrasted starkly with an overstuffed ebony chair against a wall, possibly intended for the occasional important person, albeit one with a pulse. The walls, bare of any framed picture or even a hanging calendar, provided a further starkness, as did the massive mahogany rolltop desk that almost overwhelmed the space. Only this chunk of furniture's lid, stacked along the top with medical texts like music on a spinet piano in a parlor, suggested human habitation.

A door on the left wall offered a glimpse of white cupboards and a counter above cabinets, everything looking quite sterile as if the dead might otherwise catch something. The little Charlie Chaplin-mustached assistant coroner who sat at the desk reading *The Police Gazette* looked up at Spade, recognized him with a nod and pointed toward an open door on the facing wall. This revealed a waiting-room row of restaurant-type chairs not unlike the one Spade had been tied into not so long ago.

That area was obviously for possible relatives or perhaps a friend to be brought in to identify the remains of a potential loved one. But right now the only mourners weren't mourners at all but two police detectives Spade knew too well.

Spade's friend, big barrel-chested Sergeant Tom Polhaus, sat overwhelming one of the spindle chairs, hunching with his left elbow on a knee, and the remains of a burning cigar in the fingertips of his right hand. Spade's sometime adversary, the compactly built Lieutenant Dundy, was pacing expectant-father style, like this was a place of birth, not death. Seeing Spade come in froze him, as if a doctor had arrived with bad news.

Tom, in topcoat and fedora over an indifferently pressed brown suit, stood with an embarrassed smile making a half-moon in a carelessly shaved ruddy face. He dropped his stogie to the marble floor and ground it out.

Rather shyly, he said, "Thanks for coming, Sam."

Dundy threw his sergeant a disapproving glance and said to Spade, "Someone we want you to take a look at. See if he looks familiar."

"I'm going to guess," Spade said, "you can't just ask him for his name."

The Lieutenant was as well-pressed as his sergeant was not; an open topcoat revealed a blue silk tie striped orange and white with a five-dollar gold-piece for a stickpin. A lapel of his dark grey suit bore a diamond-set Masonic emblem. The square face had been affixed somehow on a round head where short hair and a mustache bore a grey, naturally grizzled look that good grooming couldn't defeat.

Green eyes hard and accusatory, Dundy looked up at the taller Spade, who'd planted himself in front of the officer.

"He's about as anonymous as they come," Dundy said. "Got pulled out of the bay with no wallet or jewelry or identification of any kind."

"And yet you thought of me," Spade said. "I'm flattered."

"Pockets were inside out and he didn't have a dime on him."

"This is where Sherlock Holmes would figure out it was a robbery. Or maybe that a snake came down a rope and did it."

The Lieutenant did not appreciate Spade's humor. "Mind taking a look at him?" Somehow the question coming from Dundy sounded like a threat.

Spade stretched his arms in a yawn. "Love to. I mean, I came all this way. You haven't interrupted anything but a good night's sleep."

Dundy's mouth twitched and the mustache went along for the ride. His expression not quite a scowl, he motioned for Spade to follow him and Spade did, the sergeant falling in alongside his friend.

Tom whispered to Spade, "Be good, Sam."

"You know me, Tom," Spade said quietly.

"That's the trouble."

The three men moved through the uninhabited waiting area, past the long row of spindle-backed chairs and by a drinking fountain between a MEN'S and LADIES', then down a flight of metal stairs into darkness cut only by a few stingily spaced overhead yellowish bulbs. As they went clanging down, the air became increasingly moist and musty; at the bottom a cement wall with a metal door awaited them, where Dundy—obviously a regular visitor to these near-dark quarters—pushed some electric light buttons.

Dundy used a key on the lock of the big heavy metal door and drew it open, then motioned Spade and Tom into a chilly room and followed them in. Thanks to the buttons Dundy had pushed, they were met by overhead white lighting, two bright rows of bare bulbs screwed into the ceiling of this white-walled chamber. Two walls of morgue lockers faced each other, and the shorter wall at the far end bore more of the compartments, all in a space that was barely eight feet wide.

The lieutenant shut the door behind them with an ominous clunk.

Spade frowned, nostrils twitching at the sickly sweet antiseptic aroma of formaldehyde. "We just going to look at random stiffs," he said, "or did you have someone specific in mind?"

A little smile formed under Dundy's grizzled mustache, but it had scant to do with the usual reasons for smiling.

He went to a specific locker that came to his breast, unlatched its square door and pulled on the tray's rounded edge; roller bearings slid the contents out to him—a male body with no sheet covering it.

"Well?" Dundy said to Spade.

The Lieutenant stood on one side of the rolled-out tray and Spade and Tom on the other.

"Average build," Spade said with a shrug. "Maybe five nine. Bit on the hairy side. Eastern European? Not particularly athletic, but in decent shape, for a dead guy. Any tattoos?"

"No, Sam," Tom said, the small dark eyes shrewd in a thick-featured face. He was a better man than his lieutenant thought. "No notable birthmarks, either."

Dundy's piercing green eyes were fixed on Spade, not the corpse. "Anybody you know, Spade?"

"No," Spade said. He shot the Lieutenant a mockingly pleasant expression. "Anybody *you* know, Dundy?"

A sneer lifted half of Dundy's grey mustache. "If I did, would I have bothered you?"

"Probably, if you thought there was anything in it." Spade came around to Dundy's side of the tray and looked right at the Lieutenant as he said in a voice colder than the room: "Can I go now?"

Dundy said, with mild sarcasm, "Anything you'd like to share, before you leave us?" He gestured to the corpse, whose open eyes stared up at nothing. "Anything your professional skills as a detective might tell you?"

"If you pulled him from the Bay," Spade said, going along with the request but not bothering to take another look at the deceased, "he wasn't in it long. Not a hint of bloating. No biting from hungry salmon or halibut that I can see, or those midget sharks out there. He's in pretty decent shape for a stiff."

Dundy said, "I could have Tom turn him over on his belly for you and you could get a look at where he *isn't* in such good shape."

"Oh?"

The Lieutenant nodded. "Somebody bashed his head in. And it wasn't a salmon or halibut or even a shark. Care to see?"

Spade waved the suggestion away. "Don't go to any trouble on my account."

Dundy got a terrible smile going. He rolled the dead man back into his cubbyhole and slammed the locker door, latched it. "We'll call it quits for now, Spade…*if* you'll answer a question or two. We can do it here or go up to my office in the Hall of Justice. It's just next door."

His tone bland, his eyes taking on the dreamy look he often hid behind, Spade said, "Here'll do fine, unless it's going to take a while. I'm a working man. I need my rest."

Dundy batted that away. "We can do this here. Really, it's just one thing. You're, uh, nosing into this Maltese falcon business again, we understand. Talking to that Cairo queer and the O'Shaughnessy dame in stir. Asking around about this and that in the Russian sections. Dropping by to see Chicago gamblers at hotels. You led us to believe that black statue affair was a closed book."

"I thought it was."

"What opened it?"

"I have a client with an interest. That's all."

"Is it?"

Spade drew in cold air and let it out. "Come on, Dundy. Haven't you ever had a case that wouldn't let hold of you? That everybody around you said was yesterday's news but it still kept cropping up?"

"I have," Dundy admitted.

Spade pointed a finger at the world outside the morgue. "Well, that goddamn bird is still out there. And I wouldn't mind finding it and really closing the damn book."

Tom took a step closer and said, "Don't tell me you're getting obsessed with that thing, too, Sam! Look what little good it did the fat man and all his crooked cronies."

"I'm not obsessed," Spade said blandly, "I've just had my

interest piqued. And I'll level with you—I have more than one client in this thing."

Dundy spoke through his teeth. "Who, damnit!"

"My attorney informs me I do not have to share my clients' names with you guardians of the public good. It's a matter of client confidentiality. I mention it only to inform you that I have every legal right to continue my investigation into the whereabouts of that particular *rara avis*. That means 'rare bird,' by the way."

Dundy's face hardened; the green eyes took on a nasty glitter as he looked at Spade but addressed Tom. "I'll tell you what this bedroom dick's obsessed with, Sergeant—making a killing. The financial kind."

Spade scowled at the cop. "You're not as smart as you look, Dundy. In fact I would say you are pretty goddamn dumb. I'll let you know when you figure me out, which will be a week from never."

Dundy got almost nose to nose with Spade, part of it due to the cramped quarters, part of it not. He thumped Spade on the chest and was about to make a point when the private eye grabbed the cop's wrist and said through his teeth, "Didn't I tell you what I'd do if you put your goddamned paws on me again?"

Spade shoved the police lieutenant, hard, with a single thick-fingered hand, and the smaller man stumbled back into the wall of morgue lockers. The latch handle on one caught the officer in the back and he grimaced.

Face reddening, Tom said, "Aw, Sam…"

"I didn't mean to hurt the son of a bitch," Spade said, although that was not clearly the case.

Dundy steadied himself and looked at Spade with a new ferocity, then came at him, bull-like, with both fists at the ready. Spade caught him with a flat hand against the chest, his left, his right a fist now, ready to deliver a blow that would keep the promise of his sloping shoulders and his frowning satanic features.

"You hitting a citizen is going to put Tom on the spot, Dundy," Spade said, his smile wolfish, his yellow-grey eyes not at all dreamy now.

The Lieutenant was shaking under Spade's straight-arm palm.

Spade went on: "Because when I hit you, you'll lose teeth, and you'll have a story to tell down at the lodge that'll either be embarrassing or a goddamn lie."

"Polhaus will back me up," Dundy said, wriggling under Spade's palm like an insect under a pin, and his composure, his poise, were nowhere in sight. "And you'll have struck an officer of the law!"

"Please leave me out of this," Tom said, holding up his hands like a suspect under arrest.

With quiet menace, breathing hard, Spade said to Dundy, "Yeah, well your buddy Bryan, our esteemed D.A.? Reminded me I'm an officer of the court, so neither one of us will come out of this smelling like a rose. But if they take my license, Dundy, I'll sue the city and we'll be all over the front page of the *Call* and my business will improve and you'll look like a fool and we'll find out if the Police Commissioner will relish the black eye this little dust-up will cause his department."

The red-faced Tom said to his superior, "Take it easy, Lieutenant."

Dundy stopped wriggling; it was gradual but he stopped. His voice was as soft as his words were hard: "Your day will come, Spade."

The wolfish smile returned, an awful variety of the thing. "Maybe. But not today. Not tonight. Not in front of all these witnesses."

Spade tossed his head toward the wall of lockers behind

him. In back of Dundy, his sergeant had to stop himself smiling.

"Let's…let's forget it," Dundy said, embarrassed now. "I had a long day. Not that that excuses it."

Spade might have been somewhat embarrassed himself. "I had a long one, too."

Reasonable and borderline emotional, Dundy said, "Just tell me one thing, Spade. Give me one honest answer. All I ask."

Spade's breathing was normal now. "I'm listening."

Dundy pointed to the locker within which the dead man lay. "That fit fellow in there, spread out in all his glory—does he have anything to do with all that Maltese falcon malarkey?"

"No," Spade said.

"No, or 'no' as far as you know?"

"As far as a person knows, Dundy, is all anybody can know."

Dundy pulled in some of the icy air and let it out; if it had been any colder his breath would've been visible. "Then that's all, Spade. No more questions for now." He tasted his tongue and didn't seem to like it. Then he said quietly: "Shake on it?"

"Sure," Spade said, and they shook hands. He and Tom shook, too. The ritual seemed to cool things down; but the heat of it remained, underneath.

Upstairs, just outside the pebbled glass-and-wood door of the Coroner's Office, Tom stopped Spade.

"Sorry about all this, Sam," Tom said.

Spade gave his friend's shoulder a playful shove. "You should be, Tom. Rousting me out of my bed to come over and play John L. Sullivan with your boss. What was the idea, anyway, asking me to identify some random floater?"

"Take it easy, Sam. Nothing random about it."

Tom dug in his topcoat pocket and came back with an envelope marked EVIDENCE. From it the detective sergeant withdrew a small, moist item: a business card.

"That was in the dead man's topcoat pocket," Tom said.

The business card bore a familiar address, and the words SPADE & ARCHER.

CHAPTER NINE
The Little Sister

Spade dragged into his office just past four P.M. after a day canvassing the Russian enclave south of Sutter Street, again getting no leads on the whereabouts of the elusive General Kemidov. He found Effie Perine seated behind her desk and on the telephone. She looked up at him with big startled brown eyes and covered the candlestick receiver with a red-nailed hand.

She whispered, "You're going to want to take this, Sam."

Spade shut the door behind him as Effie returned to her phone conversation to say cheerily, "He's just come in, Miss Wonderly."

Spade blinked at that—"Wonderly" was the likely phony last name Brigid O'Shaughnessy had used when she first came to the Spade & Archer agency. He went over and sat on the edge of his secretary's desk, taking the phone receiver she handed him. Effie Perine watched and listened, a pretty young woman in a simple yellow frock, curiosity bursting, wavy light-brown hair crowding her chin.

"This is Sam Spade.... Yes, I recognize your name, Miss Wonderly.... I'd be happy to.... Yes, now is good.... The Coronet apartments? Fine.... See you in half an hour."

Spade hung up the receiver and sat perched on the desk with his arms folded, amusement exaggerating the V of his lips. "Well, I'll be damned. You know who that was, angel?"

"I know who she said she was," Effie Perine said. "But that doesn't seem possible."

"Corrine Wonderly," Spade said, shaking his head, sliding off onto his Florsheims. "The kid sister Brigid O'Shaughnessy said was in the clutches of Floyd Thursby."

A skeptical smile tweaked a corner of the sunburned girl's pretty mouth. "How many last names do these Wonderly women have?"

"Three, that I know of," Spade said, going to the door. Halfway out, he said, "The interesting thing? The deceptive Miss O'Shaughnessy claimed to have made the girl up out of thin air. Lock up at six, would you? See if you can get those letters typed before you go."

"That's already done."

Spade gave her a magnanimous wave. "Then go on home at five. Be sure to tell your Ma what a wonderful boss you have."

"She already knows," his secretary said with some tease in her voice.

The Coronet Apartment Hotel was on California Street, in the heart of Nob Hill, far enough from Spade's office for him to take a streetcar. The building, barely a year old, was seventeen sleek stories fronted by an ornate, sculpted facade that belied its otherwise modern look. The doorman, done up enough to appear in a Gilbert and Sullivan operetta, was expecting Spade, and called ahead to inform Miss Wonderly of the detective's arrival.

Corrine Wonderly was camped out, at the moment anyway, in apartment 1001, where after a familiar ride up, Spade knocked.

The young woman who answered, cracking the door half open, did not strikingly resemble Brigid O'Shaughnessy, being neither tall nor slender but of medium height, and curvaceous in a Clara Bow way. The matching blouse and pleated skirt caught the pastel blue of her cloche hat, from under which curled a more auburn shade of red hair than that of her incarcerated sibling's; nor were the big blue eyes of her sister's cobalt shade. The two young women had little in common other than striking beauty.

"So you're Sam Spade," she said. Something little-girl lingered in her rather high-pitched voice.

"And you're Corrine Wonderly," Spade said. "Or is it O'Shaughnessy? Or maybe LeBlanc. Your sister seems to have no shortage of surnames. If she is your sister."

"It's Wonderly," she said, a trifle embarrassed if also amused. "And, yes, she is my sister. Would you come in?" She asked this as if he were someone who had just dropped by and not been summoned.

Spade stepped inside the familiar suite—he'd been here several times recently, before this girl's sister had moved into a County Jail #1 cell—and removed his fedora, setting it on a table by the door; he wore no topcoat.

The apartment was modern, appointed in tones of red and cream, and rather good-sized with a small kitchen, bathroom, and two bedrooms. In the generous sitting room, Corrine Wonderly settled herself into a ruby-cushioned walnut settee while Spade took a brocaded oval-backed chair opposite.

Spade leaned forward. "Your sister told me two interesting things about you, Miss Wonderly."

"Is that so? And please call me Corrine. May I call you Sam or do you prefer Samuel?"

"Sam's fine. No one but Mother Spade calls me 'Samuel.' "

Her smile, bee-stung and red-rouged, showed amusement but also interest, hands folded in her lap, knees primly together, small feet snugged into baby-blue Mary Janes.

Corrine Wonderly asked, "And what are those two interesting things that Brigid told you about me?"

Spade leaned back, crossed his arms and settled his right ankle above his left knee. "First, that you ran off impulsively with Floyd Thursby, a notorious gangster or something, and she wanted the Spade and Archer agency to help get you back. Second, a bit later, that all of that was just a load of hooey to get either my late partner or myself brought in unawares to be a sort of protector for your sister, to get this Thursby character dealt with. Oh, and also that you in fact did not exist. Which you seem to."

"She can be such a liar, my sister," the girl said, and crossed her arms as well. "But I do love her. She does have some good qualities."

"I'm sure." Spade's eyes took on their dreamy look, his mouth a smile that wasn't quite a smirk. "What do you want me to do? I'd prefer we pass up the phony-story step and go straight to the truth."

"In some respects," Corrine Wonderly said with a little shrug, "you may well know more than I."

"I'll let you know when we overlap."

"Thank you." Her light blue eyes looked inward. "We were raised in New York, upstate, not the city. Our father was, and is, a real estate agent."

Spade said, "You can skip the part about the log cabin you girls were born in and get to the heart of it."

"All right," the girl said with a fleeting, mildly embarrassed smile. Then she dove right back in: "I was always the meek one, and a bit of an ugly duckling, I'm afraid."

"You turned out fine. Go on."

"Brigid, well, she was sort of the eternal wild child. Boys and cars and bathtub gin."

"Girls will be girls."

The young woman held up her small hands as if she were in

a street-corner robbery. "Oh, I know Brigid puts on a refined front. Not difficult for her, because we really do come from money. Not big money, but, uh, money nonetheless."

"Good for you."

Her eyes narrowed. "You're something of a tease, aren't you, Sam?"

Spade let some air out and his grin became relaxed. "No, I've just had a long day. Did you have anything to do with this Floyd Thursby business?"

The Wonderly girl shook her head; curls along the edges of the cloche hat bounced fetchingly. "Not directly. I got a call from Brigid, at home—I still live with our parents, who right now are vacationing in Europe..."

Spade leaned an elbow on the armrest. "Your sister mentioned that. I frankly didn't know if it was true. Didn't even know if there actually were any parents in this thing."

Corrine Wonderly shook her head again. "Oh, they're alive and well, but they don't haven't anything to do with any of this."

The detective's eyes narrowed. "Excuse me, Miss Wonderly, but...with what?"

"I'm getting to that," the girl insisted. "Brigid brought me in—she was staying at the St. Mark—and told me all about it."

Spade shifted in the chair; her vagueness seemed to be getting to him. "Please be specific."

"By 'it,' " the young woman said, trying to sound offhand, "I mean this Maltese falcon business."

Spade leaned in. "What was your role to be?"

Her shoulders went up and came down. "Brigid didn't explain that fully. But she did say it was going to mean a great deal of money which she would share with me. We were—we are—very close, actually."

Spade frowned thoughtfully. "Have you visited her at the lock-up?"

"I tried." Her jaw was firm. "I intend to keep trying."

Spade waved that off. "I may be able to help on that score, but go ahead with your story."

The girl shrugged. "There isn't much more to it. Brigid introduced me to a retired military man, a Russian, a general I think."

Spade frowned again. "Kemidov?"

"Yes." The bee-stung lips parted to let out a near whisper. "This is a shade embarrassing, but…Brigid said this general had an eye for young women, particularly of a fairly tender age…under eighteen. I'm twenty, but Brigid said I would 'pass.' "

Spade considered her with a frankly appraising glance. "You would indeed. What did Brigid want from Kemidov?"

The girl leaned forward, hands clasped. "My sister suspected the general might have a certain object, this valuable falcon thing-a-ma-jig." Her eyes turned away from his. "I was to…this is embarrassing, but…I'm sorry."

Spade's words came out casual, nonjudgmental. "You were to seduce him."

Corrine Wonderly drew air in deep and let it out slowly before confirming the detective's assumption. "That's what Brigid wanted of me. I refused, we argued, but then she said all I had to do was…'play up' to the general and that should be enough. I frankly don't know specifically what my sister had in mind. Brigid said she was on another track to get the falcon, but had suspicions about this Russian general and my job was to learn if he in fact still had the statuette. She suspected a switch had been made."

The yellow-grey eyes weren't dreamy at all now. "And did you learn this from the general?"

With a slight huffiness, the girl said, "Well, I never seduced him, but he certainly tried to…seduce me. And yes, I did manage to pry certain information from him."

"Go on."

"I learned that General Kemidov had the falcon, but by that time Brigid had been arrested and I frankly was beside myself, with no idea what to do."

She began to cry. Spade joined her on the settee and slipped an arm around her shoulders; then she wept into his nearest one.

"I stayed at the St. Mark," the girl said softly, in a confessional manner, "awaiting instructions, ready for any word from her. Nothing came. I knew Brigid had moved here, to this apartment, and I had a key she'd given me, so I moved in, figuring she'd get in touch somehow…but she didn't."

"Miss O'Shaughnessy was a busy girl last week," Spade observed. "And after that, under lock and key."

Her face, young and pretty and tear-streaked, lifted itself to look up at Spade as if an offering. "I stayed here…tucked away, waiting for whatever she might ask me to do…hoping it wouldn't be too demanding or unpleasant. You never knew with Brigid."

"You never do," Spade agreed.

Corrine Wonderly swallowed. "And then of course I started seeing all of these things, these disturbing things, in the newspapers, including your partner's murder.…Brigid had mentioned you, Sam, a private detective she'd hired for protection, as this valuable artifact she was seeking had attracted all sorts of…disreputable types."

"It had indeed. It still is."

Her head shook slowly. "With my sister arrested for murder, I didn't know what to think. I considered contacting Mama and Papa overseas, but they are due home soon anyway and…frankly, what would I tell them? That their older daughter was accused of killing the partner of a detective she'd hired to protect her from…oh, it was just too much! Too much."

"So you decided to call my office."

Her nod was firm though tears continued to trickle down her lovely cheeks. "I did. Now that she's imprisoned and may be facing life behind bars or even the gallows and…"

The girl began to sob. He drew her close, held her, patted her, dried her eyes with a handkerchief. Soon she calmed.

Then he asked her, as if saying *I love you*: "Where is Kemidov?"

Her chin quivered. "I don't know…but somewhere in the city, surely. I saw him late last week, while a lot of what you and Brigid were involved in was going on."

"Where?"

"We met for lunch at the Russian Tea Room."

Spade's laugh was curt and bitter. "Well, I don't think he's been there since…I've been looking for him in every Russian nook and cranny in San Francisco for a couple of days now."

Corrine Wonderly drew gently away and gazed at him with a renewed poise. "That's what I want you to do for me, Mr. Spade. Sam. Find General Kemidov. That's the path to finding this valuable whatever-it-is."

The wolfish grin came out. "So you're after it, too, the golden dingus. It's a sickness. A contagious one."

She shook her head so hard the cloche hat nearly came off. "You don't understand. I don't want the money for myself—I want it for my sister's defense. I want to hire her the best defense attorney in all of San Francisco."

Spade cocked his head. "You said your folks were well off. When they get back—"

Her sigh was almost a groan. "They've already disowned her. Brigid got into so much trouble a while back, they'd simply had enough, their patience exhausted. That's where the name 'O'Shaughnessy' comes from."

Spade didn't follow that. "Where does it come from?"

"He was her husband. Declan O'Shaughnessy."

"Was? They divorced?"

Her smile was a nervous thing that was barely even a smile. "No, Brigid, uh…well, she *may* have murdered him. She says not, though. People tend to think the worst of her."

The V's of Spade's eyebrows flattened out over the yellow-grey orbs. "I can see that. 'May have' murdered him, you say…?"

As matter-of-factly as she could manage, Corrine Wonderly said, "He was an older man, a banker in town. Walked out on his wife, an older woman, for Brigid, who was, after all…younger. She may not have been faithful—I can't really say. If so, who could blame her? He drank. He was violent. One night he came home and she, uh, mistook him for a prowler and shot him."

"Everybody makes mistakes."

The young woman was adamant. "He was a terrible husband. And the worst of it is, he left all his money to his grown children. If Brigid was going to plan his murder, wouldn't she have had a look at his will first? So surely she must have been innocent."

Spade's eyes went wide. "Innocent isn't a word that often applies to your sister, but let's stay on track. You want me to find Kemidov, which I'm glad to do for you…for a fee starting with a modest retainer."

This surprised her. "How, uh…modest?"

"Five C's should do it."

"You mean—five hundred dollars?"

"Yes. Against fifty dollars a day, capped at a grand."

Hysteria leapt in the blue eyes. "That's a little high, isn't it?"

"Not when at least three people have been shot dead in this thing so far."

If she'd frowned any harder, all of the prettiness would have gone out of her features. But she didn't and it didn't. "But you were looking for Kemidov already!"

Spade wagged a finger at her. "You only want me to find Kemidov so you can get your pretty little hands on the Maltese falcon. Don't kid me, sister."

Her chin came up. "What if we split fifty-fifty on whatever the artifact realizes? How about that?"

The wolfish grin came out again, woken from its cave. "If you can help me find Kemidov, we'll forget the retainer and just go into business together. I can even recommend a good defense attorney for you to fund for your sister, a gent called Sid Wise. You'll love him. First, you'll have to help me out."

"What do you need from me?"

Their eyes were locked now.

"I'm at a dead end where Kemidov is concerned," Spade said. "Any leads at all would help. I don't even know what this Russian general of ours looks like, other than the vaguest physical description your sister gave me."

Corrine Wonderly thought about that. "Would a photograph help?"

"Of course."

The girl scurried from the sitting room into one of the bedrooms and soon returned with a photograph in hand—a snapshot taken outdoors, possibly in a park—of her sister and a smiling man with a well-trimmed beard and a full head of dark hair, average size and in a nice-looking double-breasted topcoat. At his side, Brigid wore a stylish fall coat and was smiling too, wearing a typically beautiful expression.

Like the pair in the photo, Spade was smiling but in a cat-that-ate-the-canary way as he returned the photo to Corrine Wonderly, who looked at him curiously.

"I can tell you," Spade said, "exactly where to find Kemidov—no charge."

"Wonderful!" the Wonderly girl said. "Where? But finding him may not be enough. I may still need you in my employ, for protection."

"Maybe, maybe not."

If she'd moved any closer to him on the settee, she'd have been in his lap.

"Where is he, Mr. Spade?"

"Sam, remember?"

"Sam. Where?"

"The City Morgue. He's on ice."

She drew away in shock, her eyes wide, her mouth wide.

"Saw him there myself, last night," Spade clarified. "Couldn't identify him then, but now I can."

The young woman began to shiver, the big blue eyes moving in thought, and tucked herself back under his arm.

Spade consoled her: "There, there. Everything will be fine."

"Should I…go to the police about this? Or…the morgue and make a proper identification?"

"No, honey. My advice? Take the next train back to wherever it is in upstate New York you're from, and wait for your folks to get back home."

Small white teeth came together and she spoke through them, right at him. "But I want that falcon, Sam! I need the money to get that defense attorney for my sister!"

"We still have a deal," Spade assured her. He touched her face, her cheek, with tenderness. "But I'm not crazy about having you underfoot. Too many people have died in this thing already. I don't want you to be one of them. You go home and I'll get in touch with you there."

The girl clutched him. "You don't even know me, Mr. Spade!

How can you claim to care about me? Who are you trying to kid?"

Spade leaned in and gave her a kiss; not a fierce thing but a real kiss by any definition. Some of her lip rouge was on his mouth when he finished.

"We'll call that the retainer," he said, wiping off the red with a handkerchief, and stuffed it away, got up, put on his hat, touching its brim to her, and went out.

CHAPTER TEN
Another Client

The next morning, coming in just after eight in a vested suit but no topcoat, Spade greeted Effie Perine with a weary smile. She met it with uplifted eyebrows and a modest grin.

"More Russian kick dancing today, Sam?"

The young tawny-haired girl was in a pink and white dress today and looked fresh and cheery.

Spade slung his hat on the coat tree. "It's called a Prisyadka, my dotty darling. And, no—that line of inquiry is shut down."

"How come?"

He sat on the edge of her desk and told her about his trip to the morgue the night before, and how the man on a cold slab had been a cold Kemidov.

"Oh dear," Effie Perine said. "Are you going to tell the police?"

"I'd like to keep it to myself, but maybe. I'll talk to Sid Wise about it."

"Your attorney. Good idea." Her boyish brow squinted in thought. "If the Russian neighborhoods are nix now, Sam, what next?"

He slipped off her desk. "Your boss is too much of an ignoramus himself to be sure." He yawned, stretched. "Let me know if any paying customers drop by."

"Will do," she said, as Spade passed her on the way to his inner sanctum. Before he hit the light switch, he glanced at the Christmas tree, which now bore several strands of glowing flame-shaped electric lights, red and blue and green. Spade shook his head and smiled a little.

"The rattle-brained little angel," he said to himself with a chuckle, then got behind the big scarred yellow desk and into the swivel-chair. A balmy breeze was plumping the buff drapes on the slightly open windows behind him.

He stared at nothing and without looking plucked a drawstring pouch of Bull Durham tobacco from one vest pocket and cigarette papers and lighter from the other. He selected a paper from its packet, which he returned to its nesting place before sifting tobacco into a curve of that paper, his thick fingers shaping the cigarette as if of their own deft volition. He licked the cigarette shut, twisted its ends, then placed it between his lips and fired it with the lighter. He drew deep on the roll-your-own.

"Merry Christmas, Miles," Spade said softly to his absent and very dead partner through a wreath of expelled smoke. "I should have buried you under that goddamned tree."

Effie Perine almost caught him talking to himself. Spade, not easily startled, was.

"Yes, sweetheart?" he said, and coughed cigarette smoke.

Her brown eyes were big, her vocal volume small. "You won't believe this, Sam."

"You might be surprised what I'd believe."

The girl jerked a thumb over her shoulder as if she were hitchhiking. "You do have a walk-in customer," she whispered. "And does he look like money."

Spade sat up, his smile wolfish, the yellow-grey eyes alert. "Well, you know what to do, precious. Send him in. Send him in..."

The detective rested his cigarette in the brass ashtray and got to his feet. Effie Perine held open the connecting door and the prospective client entered, a well-made man whose presence was immediately formidable, in a gentlemanly brown herringbone suit with waistcoat and black-and-white necktie snugged at the starched white collar of a light tan shirt. His utterly bald head was compensated by a full black mustache, his features languidly handsome. In one leather-gloved hand was a silver-handled hardwood cane, in the other, at his side, a dark brown homburg. Tucked under his left arm was a slender dispatch case of dark leather.

"Mr. Spade," a resonant, British-accented voice began, "Steward Blackwood. I do apologize for just arriving like this. I realize I really should have called first. But I do have my reasons for limiting my…exposure."

"No apology necessary." Spade gestured to the oaken client's chair across from his desk. "Please have a seat, Mr. Blackwood. What can I do for you?"

Steward Blackwood sat and placed his homburg carefully on the yellow desktop, avoiding the faint scattering of grey cigarette ash near the brass tray and respecting the near edge of the green desk blotter. The dignified man spent several seconds getting that just right. He leaned his cane against the desk and positioned the dispatch case on his lap. The lights on the Christmas tree nearby outlined an edge of him.

Spade swung slightly in the swivel-chair, to face his visitor, who glanced at the cigarette burning in the tray and said to his host, "You may smoke, sir," as if Spade had asked permission.

Then the visitor removed from an inner coat pocket a brown leather three-finger cigar case with cutter. With as much ritualistic care as Spade routinely brought to his rolling of cigarettes, Steward Blackwood selected a cigar, clipped its end and lighted up. The masculinely fragrant smoke from the cigar wafted, caught by the partially open window to Spade's back, as buff curtains trembled.

The prospective client leaned back in the oaken chair as if it were comfortable and got his cigar going, his eyes not on Spade. The lack of eye contact did not speak of awkwardness. The two men might have been in a drawing room somewhere, seated in a quiet atmosphere of male relaxation and satisfactory digestion.

"I have read of your involvement, sir," Steward Blackwood said finally, the mellowness of his voice fighting the formality of his words, "in this unfortunate Maltese falcon affair. Of course, I'm sure the newspapers have, as is their practice, exaggerated the tragic circumstances."

"Not really," Spade said. "Multiple homicides require little exaggeration."

The visitor sighed rich smoke. "Nonetheless, I'm sure they provided what they might call 'color.' I mention this not only to lay the groundwork for a conversation that grows out of that affair, but to explain that I am here not on referral but due to your involvement in, again, the matter of this rather valuable artifact."

Spade collected his cigarette from the brass tray and returned the damp cylinder to his lips, with his tone less polite now as he replied: "What is your interest in the matter, Mr. Blackwood, beyond curiosity aroused by newspaper accounts?"

The man's eyebrows were bushy little echoes of his mustache; they rose over the otherwise placid features. "I represent the legal owners of the Maltese falcon."

"Oh."

A leather-gloved hand gestured. "Or perhaps I should say *the* owner. One never knows whether to refer to a museum in the singular or the plural, particularly one of the scale of the British Museum."

Spade let some white smoke out and returned his roll-your-own to the brass tray. "When you say the British Museum, you don't mean *a* British museum, but, as you put it…*the*?"

His smile and his nod were slight. "You are correct, sir. And I am *an* assistant curator, not *the* assistant curator. We have over sixty galleries. Currently, I am in the United States..."

"So I noticed." Spade spoke with a mild edge of growing irritation.

"...dealing with certain artifacts we are acquiring or that have been donated to us. I specialize in Colonial Period antiquities, predating your revolution."

"The Maltese falcon is neither American," Spade pointed out, "nor an artifact of Colonial America."

Steward Blackwood gestured casually with a gloved hand holding his burning cigar. "Obviously. This is an unusual circumstance to say the least, one in which an individual of your qualifications and I might say skills are uniquely suited."

"I hope that's a compliment."

"It certainly is. Again, in these circumstances, it is. Circumstances which would best be described as criminal but not in such a way that going through the authorities, either local or federal, would be desirable. Your local police, meaning no disrespect, are not immune from, let us say, temptation. And your Bureau of Investigation on the federal level has a rather poor reputation. Again, meaning no disrespect."

Spade's cigarette dangled from his lips and he sat back with arms folded. "The local cops in this burg are no more corrupt than the next department their size—maybe a little less so. But, no, they aren't immune from temptation. And the Bureau of Investigation is a bunch of chumps. That's American for trigger-happy idiots."

A smile formed around the cigar as the assistant curator took in Spade's words.

"I believe," Steward Blackwood said, "I came to the right person."

"That will depend," Spade said.

"Oh?"

"On what it is you want me to do. I will tell you right now that you are not the first person, the first client, to approach me regarding the bona fide falcon, which is, after all, still missing."

"Before we go further," the assistant curator said, and wrestled briefly with the attaché case on his lap, withdrawing a sheaf of papers, "you should familiarize yourself with these… which are yours to keep, mimeograph copies, though for now I suggest you go over them quickly. That should be sufficient to our momentary needs."

Spade looked the four stapled mimeographed sheets over. The documents indicated that the museum had acquired the falcon legally from General Kemidov at a price of thirty-five thousand pounds sterling. Attached was the bill of sale from a Parisian antiques shop for 100 francs dating to 1911.

Spade, clearly amused, flipped through the pages. "So the dingus brought about twenty U.S. dollars less than twenty years ago."

"If by 'dingus' you refer to the Maltese falcon, yes," the assistant curator said. "It changed hands many times between apparently casual buyers, all of whom seem to have taken it for nothing more than a moderately interesting black enamel statuette."

"As I presume the British Museum does not," Spade said, "now that it's known to be made of solid gold and jewel-encrusted. I'm guessing your people will be pretty fussy about how they remove that black lacquer coat."

The hand with the cigar gestured casually, but the assistant curator's eyes were hard, dark, gleaming. "They—we—will be circumspect indeed…if we have the opportunity. And we did have it in our hands, our possession, including those of our experts, long enough to thoroughly authenticate it."

"Even if it can't be authenticated," Spade said, the V's of his eyebrows flattening, "a chunk of gold with fabulous rubies and emeralds and sapphires is plenty valuable. I think you fellas got a bargain."

"No," Steward Blackwood said crisply, "all we got was swindled."

"How so?"

The sigh had a wealth of cigar smoke in it but even more frustration. "Our 'bargain,' as you put it, with this unscrupulous Russian general, had not been sealed upon authentication. It went back into his possession while the contract was further negotiated and ultimately signed. And General Kemidov indeed delivered the falcon to us. Or I should say *a* falcon."

"A phony."

The assistant curator's nod was one of resignation. "A copy, yes. And, based upon the newspaper accounts I referred to earlier, the Russian seems to have had a number of such black-enamel copies made."

"Lead and black enamel," Spade corrected.

Steward Blackwood's upper lip curled in half a sneer. "The particulars of the copy, or copies, are not of interest to the British Museum. The original is." His expression hardened; froze. "We want you to bring us the genuine antiquity, Mr. Spade. It is ours. We paid for it."

Spade's expression was as cold as the assistant curator's. "Some paid for it already, with their lives. You'd have to be prepared to pay for it again with that in mind."

The shake of his head could hardly have been slower. "We are not prepared to pay anything more."

"Well, then..."

Steward Blackwood opened a gloved palm. "However…we can offer you a twenty percent finder's fee, based on the object's estimated American value of fifty thousand dollars… after a non-refundable five-hundred dollar retainer, of course."

From an inside suitcoat pocket, this latest potential client withdrew a brown leather wallet from which he withdrew five crisp one-hundred-dollar bills. He lay them before Spade on the desktop, one at a time, until they were spread out like a winning poker hand.

"As I say, non-refundable, Mr. Spade. Will that be sufficient?"

Spade's eyes were on the man, not the money. "Is that the extent of my duties? The little matter of getting you a particular solid gold jewel-studded statue?"

The assistant curator's nod was matter-of-fact. "It is, but in reality, your job, as you must surely realize, includes finding Kemidov. It's clear this damned general has the real falcon in his possession. It's also clear that he's an unscrupulous, dangerous individual. So we know what it is we're asking you to risk."

"You want me to find Kemidov. That's part of it."

The visitor spread his gloved hands. "We…I…feel finding Kemidov is finding the falcon. But that is an assumption, and we have no interest in the Russian general beyond recovery of what we legally acquired from him. He can live or die as far as we are concerned. Having negotiated the purchase of the falcon myself, I admit being rather inclined toward the latter contingency."

Spade's head cocked, his mouth half-smiled. "You aren't suggesting I kill anyone."

Steward Blackwood shook his head firmly, several times. "No, no, no. Certainly not." He leaned forward, his eyes half-lidded and firm. "I am merely suggesting I have no interest in exactly how you go about recovering the Maltese falcon. All we are interested in is its return." He sat back, let out air, half-rose. "If you need to get in touch, I am at the Belvedere."

"Under your own name?"

"Certainly."

The assistant curator gathered his things, leaving only his half-smoked cigar behind in the brass tray, nodding to Spade before exiting into the outer office, granting the detective a smile as he went.

"Well," Effie Perine said, coming in after the museum man had gone, leaning in the doorway.

"Call Sid Wise and see if he's in," Spade said, frowning. "Find out if he can see me."

"When?"

"Soon as he can."

"Will do."

She went quickly back to her desk and telephone.

Spade entered a pinkish office building on the corner of Sutter and Kearny and went up to 827. He said hello to the plumply cute redhead at the switchboard and she smiled over her lacy collar. "Hello, Mr. Spade…he's expecting you—go on in."

A folder with the mimeograph copies of the museum papers under one arm, Spade headed through an underpopulated reception area into a corridor long enough to accommodate several office doors. At the end of this rather dreary passage, he knocked, then went directly through the frosted-glass door marked *Wise, Merican & Wise*.

Sid Wise, a small man at a big desk, looked up between piles of papers and briefs, brandishing a stub of a cigar as if he were directing an orchestra when all he was doing was waving Spade in. The balding attorney's skin was olive, hair thinning, face oval, shoulders dandruff-strewn. He was a millionaire in a five-dollar suit.

"Sammy," Sid Wise said, in his rather high-pitched voice, "what have you got yourself into this time?"

"Will you make a transatlantic call for me?"

The lawyer grinned around the stubby cigar in his teeth. "At random or t'somebody specific?"

Spade sat in the client chair across from the little lawyer. He removed the stapled mimeograph pages from the folder and tossed them on the desk between the towers of papers. "I want these authenticated."

Wise smirked. "I can't do that over the telephone, Sammy."

"I know how phones work," Spade said. "Send those papers by closed bag from here to New York and on to Merry Olde. But you can right away check on whether this character who came by the office today is who he says he is."

Sid Wise scratched his head and more dandruff made its way to his shoulders. "Why, do you suspect him?"

"I don't. I just want to make sure. Maybe it's that he came in and told me he got swindled and he doesn't seem like the type you could swindle."

Wise shrugged a shoulder. "One born every minute, Sammy."

"Right. I just don't want to be one of them."

When Spade didn't move out of the chair, the lawyer asked, "That all, Sammy?"

Spade shifted uncomfortably in a chair meant to encourage short stays. "Not quite," he said with obvious reluctance. "If I ask you if something I might do is illegal or not, can you answer?"

The lawyer shrugged elaborately, dandruff snowing from his shoulders onto his desk and papers stacked there. "I'm like you, Samuel Spade—an officer of a court. The answer is—it depends. Why don't you try a hypothetical?"

Spade began to make a cigarette, thinking as he went. "Okay. Hypothetically, suppose I got called to the morgue and shown a body by Dundy and Polhaus. They would like me to identify this body. And I know the corpse but don't tell them. Do not identify him. Would that be obstruction of justice?"

The small man thought about it. "Well, hypothetically—if your cop buddies didn't tell you the context, no. If they did, yes. Maybe."

Spade had a match in hand, ready to light up. "Maybe? And what do you mean, context?"

A palm extended between piles of papers and briefs. "Did they say this stiff you recognized was a murder victim, or a criminal they wanted you to identify, something clearly official?…Then maybe it's obstruction. Even so, you're not under oath."

"And if they didn't say it was official?"

"You're probably in the clear."

"And I wasn't under oath."

"Well, there you are. In the clear."

Spade, cigarette lit and dangling, was halfway out when Wise added: "Hypothetically."

CHAPTER ELEVEN
The Bríbe

Spade sat alone in a booth at John's Grill and had the 85-cent dinner, choosing the crab cocktail, clam broth, green peas and tenderloin steak options. He ate slowly, as if savoring every bite, though was actually lost in thought. During his apple pie dessert, he made a decision. In the Grill's telephone booth, he called the Alexandria Hotel and asked for a certain guest.

The phone rang a while and he had just decided she must have stepped out when she answered.

"Yes?" Rhea Gutman's voice was warm but tentative, as if she were surprised to learn anyone knew to call her here.

"Sam Spade, Miss Gutman. I have a few things to share with you. Could we meet for a drink? The Bourbon and Branch is only a ten-minute walk from your hotel—best speak in town. And I'm close enough to the Alexandria to come collect you and we can walk together."

The receiver went silent for a few seconds, then her voice returned, not at all tentative now: "There's plenty to drink here in my suite, Mr. Spade."

Spade grinned at the phone. "Only if you stop calling me 'Mr. Spade.' That makes you sound too young to entertain a gentleman caller, and me too old to get away with pretending I am one."

Her laughter was gentle, a little waterfall ripple. "I'll be happy to entertain you…Sam. I'm your employer, aren't I? And don't you have things to report?"

"I do."

"Then please come see me. I've done nothing all day but listen to the radio and read."

"I might be able to top that."

"Come see."

He hung up, his eyes narrowing as he stepped from the booth. He muttered, "Who's flirting with who?"

Spade paid for his dinner and left fifteen cents as a tip. After collecting his hat and topcoat, he ventured into the night for the brief walk to the Alexandria. The evening had grown cool and Christmas decorations were strung on streetlamps and electric wreaths glowed in windows. A cable car clanged and a foghorn sounded. He noticed none of it, further lost in his thoughts.

When the mahogany door to Suite 12-C opened, Rhea Gutman was again framed there, as if he'd returned only a few minutes since his last visit. She wore the same neck-to-ankle yellow-and-white dressing gown Spade had last seen her in, if with several differences: her hair was not damp but in sleek blonde arcs framing her heart-shaped face, and she was fully made up, the golden-brown eyes in curled-lash settings, cheeks touched with subtle circles of deep pink rouge, lipsticked lips full and carmine red. Though this time the robe bore no dampness, its clinging quality remained, highlighting legs that were long and breasts that were pert and high, and yet this woman was nonetheless small, a child just blossomed.

Wordlessly the petite blonde vision took his hat and coat, hung them in a nearby closet as he waited, then ushered Spade into the sitting room with its tones of green and rounded furnishings, taking his arm. She escorted him to the settee they'd recently shared, depositing him at one end while she glided off to the little liquor cart.

She paused there, looked back at him. "Rum and Coke again, Mr. Spade? Sam?"

"Please."

She poured the rum generously, topped it lightly with the mixer, and brought the result in a highball glass to him.

"What are you having?" Spade asked conversationally.

"Orange juice again," Rhea Gutman said, and returned to the liquor cart to pour some from a gleaming metal cocktail shaker. Over her shoulder she said, "But with a little kick this time. Gin—vodka's so hard to get. Good vodka, anyway."

The young woman, who seemed suddenly more sophisticated than her supposedly eighteen years might indicate, was just a little drunk—apparently radio and reading hadn't been her only pastime today. She settled on the settee next to Spade, rather too close, an encroachment that received no complaint from him.

"What do you have to report to your employer, Sam?" she asked with a smile, perfect little white teeth almost glowing against the bright red lips. She offered this as if it were more witty than it was.

Spade slipped an arm behind her along the upper edge of the settee. "You already know that I talked to this gambler, Dixie Monahan."

"Yes. The one the Chicago gangsters are after."

He sipped rum-and-Coke. "What I didn't mention was that I took money from him."

The red mouth and golden-brown eyes made O's. "Oh dear."

The detective frowned, raised a palm. "You asked if anyone else had paid me in this matter, and I pled client confidentiality."

She didn't seem sure whether to be hurt or indignant. "You did."

Spade's powerful sloping shoulders rose and fell. "But you have a right to know I'm not operating in conflict with your interests. I want to be clear about that. I didn't agree to find the falcon for Monahan and then turn it over to him—merely to locate it."

She wrinkled a particularly cute nose. "That sounds a little slippery."

"I suppose." He sipped rum-and-Coke again. "Miss Gutman… Rhea…I believe you may have the best legal claim to the artifact, or as close to one as anybody has. As your father said to me, 'You might as well say it belongs to the King of Spain.' Establishing clear title to the dingus, I'm afraid, is a tricky damn deal."

Rhea's woozy frown confirmed the inebriation her hooded eyes suggested. "The falcon, you mean?"

"That's right. The fabled black bird with its jeweled stuffing on the outside."

Her eyebrows, tweaked into submission, rose high on a smooth forehead. "Well, I told you—I have the bill of sale from the Russian general to my father. It's in the hotel safe."

Spade swiveled toward her, all but staring her down. "I should probably see that document."

She blinked. "Right now?"

The question made him think. The V of his mouth tightened, then relaxed, a decision made.

"No," he said. "Not right now. If I were to see the bill of sale, and learned the date exactly, I might be asked about it under oath. Better, for now, that I not know. But the date on your bill of sale is a definite factor."

Rhea Gutman straightened. "Well, it would certainly seem so," she said. "But why do you say that?"

The detective mulled her question, sipped more of his drink.

Finally he said: "I had a visitor today. A prospective client in for a consultation."

"Don't you have those all the time?"

He met her gaze. "This consultation had to do with the Maltese falcon."

Briefly, Spade told her about Steward Blackwood and how the museum curator also wanted the detective to pursue both the Russian general and the missing artifact.

Then he got specific: "Blackwood has his own bill of sale from General Kemidov, this one made out to the British Museum, which means the Russian obviously sold the damn thing more than once. And he appears to have had more than one fake fashioned, too." Spade sighed deep. "And don't forget—our friend Wilmer Cook is still out there. Just because Monahan likely called him off doesn't mean the gunsel doesn't have his own sights set on that damn bird."

Rhea Gutman clutched his suitcoat sleeve. Her concern broke through her tipsy state. "Oh dear. What I'm putting you through, Mr. Spade. Sam."

His expression turned hopeful. "If your bill of sale predates the museum's—or anybody else's who might turn up with a claim of title—you're the rightful owner. At least as far as I can tell."

She frowned, a little steadier now. "If I can't prove my ownership, what about selling it to a private collector?"

Spade cocked his head; his yellow-grey eyes had the familiar dreamy look now. "That's the smart thing. Not precisely the legal thing, but who can talk legalities when you're dealing with something dating back hundreds of years that got itself passed from one pirate to another, one thief to another?"

Her reply had sadness in it: "Like my father."

Spade didn't sugarcoat it: "Like your father."

The young woman leaned closer. "Do you have a line on such a collector?"

Spade shrugged. "No. But Joel Cairo claims to have. And the Levantine is behind bars, wishing he could afford a top mouthpiece to spring him, or anyway get him off with a light sentence. So a deal might be made there."

Rhea Gutman seemed nearly sober now, and moved so close to him her floral perfume tweaked his nostrils. "When I saw you last, Sam, you were searching the Russian sections of the city for this General Kemidov. Did you learn anything about his whereabouts? You'd tell me if you had, wouldn't you?"

Spade uttered not a word for a good ten seconds, and did not look at her for all that time. Then, as if issuing an order, he said, "Get me another rum and Coke."

She winced at that, but said, "All…all right."

"And yourself another gin and orange juice."

The girl went to the liquor cart, more a trudge than a glide this time. Soon she returned with drinks for both of them, having managed not to spill, and sat back down gracelessly.

Spade took her right hand; it was an almost tender gesture. "I'm going to tell you something, Rhea…and no one else can know. It's going to come out eventually, but we're better off, for now, with no one else knowing."

"I'm…I'm listening."

"…General Kemidov is dead."

She withdrew her hand from his, as if she feared he might be contagious. "Oh my God! You didn't…didn't *kill* him?"

Spade's upper lip curled back and his teeth bared in a terrible example of his wolfish grin. "Goddamnit, is that all you think of me? Don't you know I'm trying to help you in this thing? That I'm just about the only one in this mess who *hasn't* killed anybody?"

At once defenseless and defensive, Rhea Gutman looked up at Spade, hands folded in her lap, a primly defiant child. "*I* haven't killed anyone either."

The detective was breathing hard. The yellow-grey eyes were boiling. "Well, I hope you haven't. But I'm reserving judgment."

Her hand went to her bosom. Her chin trembled. "How can you say that? How can you think that?"

Now she was the offended party, a state she expressed through tears, producing a hanky from a pocket of the dressing gown and burying her face in it, sobbing. Spade did not look at her.

"Two cops I know," he said after a while, still not laying eyes on her as she wept, "the ones who've been in this from the beginning, called me down to the morgue to identify a body last night. I didn't tell them it was Kemidov."

That froze her.

Then she looked up sharply, tears streaking cheeks whose cosmetic pink circles were smeared now, and her red lipstick was similarly smudged, almost as if she'd been struck in the mouth and bloodied.

Spade went on, monotone: "I've kept to myself the knowledge that our Russian is dead. But it demonstrates a couple of things. This isn't over. Maybe it hasn't even really begun. Somebody bashed the Russian's head in from behind, and if somebody did that, it might be a person he trusted, a party he was comfortable turning his back to…the way Miles Archer was comfortable having his gun tucked under his coat when a beautiful woman had him backed up down an alley."

Now Spade's words lost their monotone and became more modulated: "You're a very beautiful woman yourself, Rhea. And you seem warm, even genuine. But your father was killed in this affair, and yet you're still in it. You want the falcon now. Like everybody else. And that takes a kind of coldness."

The tears had stopped but the trembling hadn't. And her defensiveness was still on display. "It…it's my father's legacy. You know that. It's all he left me…to…to…"

Spade's look was cutting. "To remember him by?"

Rhea Gutman shook two little fists. "To live! To not be poor! Don't you know that's why people do things? It isn't greed, not really. It's surviving."

The detective was shaking his head. "Not many seem to be surviving in this affair. And maybe it isn't survival you're after, Rhea."

Her response was a cry that almost echoed in the suite: "What else could it be?"

Spade's voice had lost its cruelty and turned matter-of-fact. "It could be two things at once. You could've wanted to get close enough to that Russian to get the falcon. With your looks, you could make that happen. And then kill him for it. Because this is about more than just the object and its monetary value. Oh, that's a big part of it, all right. But there's also revenge. That's the oldest motive in the book. Hell, revenge was written in the sand before there was a book. Getting even makes the world go round. Always has. Always will."

The girl looked at him as if he were a boa constrictor with a rodent half-swallowed. "How can you say such terrible things?"

Spade didn't have time to answer before she began to cry again, to weep deep, heaving with emotion.

Acting on impulse, summoning humanity, the blond satan gathered her into his arms. "You're upset."

Tiny fists pounded on his chest, though she stayed in his embrace. "Of course I'm upset! Some people have feelings! Maybe you're some kind of special…special creature. Some awful, terrible…breed."

Spade smoothed an arc of her fair hair. "Sorry, kid. It's just that I'm at the end of my rope on this thing."

Her eyes searched his face and found something possibly human there. Then her heart-shaped face lifted itself to his long narrow one and the smear of her red mouth covered the V of his lips. Then they clutched each other close enough and hard enough to hurt and repeated the process.

"You're a little thing," he said gently.

Rhea Gutman kissed him again and he gathered her into his arms and carried her like a bride, or perhaps a slumbering child; but there were three doors, making him pause, and she had to point the way into her bedroom.

The sun had been up a while and Spade had helped himself to a shower and was dressed when she stirred, a naked young woman with milky white flesh and lovely curves spilling from under the covers as if so much beauty, however petite, couldn't be contained. She stretched her fists high and yawned, not seeming to mind the covers tumbling to her waist and exposing even more supple flesh.

"You could stay," she said.

He shook his head. "I have things to do."

She frowned. "But if the general's dead…"

Spade raised a forefinger. "Keep that to yourself, remember. I have a few cards left to play in this game. You just keep your head down. People are dying. Don't be one of them."

Rhea Gutman sat up with a carelessly arranged sheet and thin blanket around her lap. She brought her legs up and hugged them, chin on a knee, and said, "So you do care?"

He was snugging his necktie into place. "Sure I do. You're going to come into money, if I have anything to say about it. And I'm on the payroll."

The lipstick was a memory and only the little white teeth remained in a sweet crescent in the heart-shaped face, the blonde arcs tousled. "You'll continue the falcon hunt for me, then?"

"Sure." Spade shook a finger at her. "But you need to know something. If that bill of sale of yours doesn't predate the museum's, or can't be verified, I'm out."

Had she heard right? "You're what?"

"Oh-you-tee." He got into his suitcoat. "You can cozy up to Cairo in stir and work the private collector angle yourself. You don't need me for that. I'd do just about anything for you, my darling. But there's two things I won't do: get killed or go to prison."

Her facial features were all O's again. "That's your thinking? That's how you've been thinking all along?"

He chuckled to himself, tightening his belt. "Of course it is."

"Knowing that, you…you…." She gestured to herself, as if noticing for the first time she was unclothed.

"Honey," he said, "I've been bribed before."

She flew from the bed and stood before him, naked as a newborn but beautiful and a full-grown if small woman, and slapped him. It rang like a gunshot.

Spade's laugh was full-throated. "I've been slapped before, too. You can fire me, if you like. Am I fired?"

Rhea Gutman looked hurt. "N-no. I'd rather know what you're up to than not."

"Smart girl," he said, at the door to the sitting room. "You'll be hearing from me."

CHAPTER TWELVE
The First Mate

The caw of circling seagulls made dissonant music in tune with the rattle of winches loading a freighter as from somewhere came the screech of a freight car diverted onto a siding by a chugging locomotive. A cool breeze blew in off the ocean, bringing pungent aromas—coffee, copra, raw sugar, oakum, salt water, dead fish and rotting piles of this and that—quietly assaulting Spade as he walked along East Street.

Here, the detective was a tourist in a town he liked to claim as his. Opposite the giant concrete piers between the Ferry Building and Matson Line docks stretched a roughhewn necklace of waterfront "cafés"—actually speakeasies in these supposedly Dry days—alongside hotels, billiard parlors, barber shops, and clothiers. Lined along the block between Market and Mission Streets were the dives, lunchrooms, and shabby stores where seafarers and longshoremen congregated to drink, fight and fornicate.

The incongruous figure in hat and topcoat moved through the early dusk past shop windows displaying dungarees, gloves, caps, cargo hooks, and accordions. Eyes frankly studied him: Was this an easy mark to roll, or was that tall broad-shouldered figure as unafraid as he seemed? Confidence and naivete, after all, could be confused for each other—or found in tandem. He strolled by a tattoo parlor offering mostly drunken patrons a home on their arms and chests for naked cupids and equally nude glamour girls, and the inevitable rope-entwined anchors.

When Spade entered the timber-framed, brick-walled, tin-ceilinged Old Shipwreck Saloon, moving through its smoky haze, he joined a clientele that included workers scarred by years or even decades of grappling with heavy loads on piers, in holds and on decks. Such patrons were missing the odd finger or occasional eye, their remaining orbs trained on Spade in his suspiciously non-nautical garb.

The women who threaded among these seldom married, often marred men liked what they saw of the newcomer, but Spade's interest in these gaudy parodies of femininity was non-existent—skinny ones on dope, heavy ones over the hill, their clothing as garishly colorful as the flags of foreign ships. The upstairs here was reputedly a brothel, these fallen flowers among soiled workers.

Prohibition in this café was respected by serving beer in soda pop bottles and harder stuff in coffee cups, and keeping the supplies, beer kegs included, under the counter and not along the barroom mirror. Behind the battered counter, wearing an apron that had once been white, was an ex-boxer bartender, a rag in one hand, a billy club in the other. His massive head might have been a souvenir contributed by some sailor after an island trip—a coconut with husk hair and crude features drawn on a big scarred face.

"We paid this week," the bartender said, annoyed. "City and feds both."

"Just a customer," Spade said.

The detective demonstrated by sliding a fin across the bar to the still wary bartender.

"Throwing money around," the bartender said, covering the bill with a big swollen-looking paw, "can get people killed."

Spade offered up his wolfish smile, patted a topcoat pocket. "That's why I brought a gun." His shrug seemed good-natured. "Don't much care for the noisy things, but there are times."

"There are," the bartender admitted with a nod.

The five-spot paid for a mug of foamy "soda pop" as well as a response to Spade's inquiry about a regular customer of the "café." A thick pointing finger indicated a small round table toward the back where the individual Spade was seeking sat with a coffee cup before him. The burly bearded seaman in white cap, black peacoat and hickory work shirt was among the better dressed of the patrons. On the wall behind him hung a December calendar displaying a beach-perched bathing beauty preparing to drink from a bottle of Coca-Cola through a straw.

Spade approached and stopped near the empty chair across from the seagoing man.

"Connor Foley?" he asked.

"I am. Who are you?"

"Samuel Spade. I'm looking for the Connor Foley who crewed on the *Paloma*."

Spade had spent much of the afternoon asking around hiring halls and union headquarters at the City Front, the area bounded by the Embarcadero, Market, Clay, and Drumm Streets.

"I'm told you were first mate," the detective said. "A Blue Book union rep suggested I might find you here."

The dark eyes in the brown-bearded face considered that, then gestured for Spade to sit, which he did, bringing his soda pop bottle of beer along.

In a husky medium-pitched voice, perhaps the aftermath of much on-deck shouting, Connor Foley said, "I know who you are. You're the private dick in the papers, tied up in those murders."

"I like to think I tied those murders up," Spade said pleasantly, "as opposed to being tied up in them. But yes. And your Captain Jacobi was one of the murder victims."

"Dropped dead in your office, the *Call* said."

"Yes, but that makes it sound like a heart attack." Spade drank from the soda pop bottle. "Bullets did it."

The *Paloma*'s first mate looked around him. "Interestin' place, the Old Shipwreck Saloon…café, I mean." He took a good long swig from the coffee cup, then smiled, sharing yellow teeth and the occasional gold one. "Know how the place got her name?"

"No."

The seafarer drank deep from the coffee cup, set it down, then leaned forward as if sharing a deep secret. "Three-masted ship be wrecked off Alcatraz Island and gets herself towed to shore, right here, and left to rot. This very spot. Somebody cuts a hole in the side of the ship and makes a grog shop out of it."

"Must have been thirsty."

A callused hand painted a picture in the air. "Over time, the ship gets swallowed up by mud and crud, and damn near of her own free will, this very building goes up over her." Connor Foley leaned back and folded his arms. "And that, Mr. Samuel Spade, is all you get out of Connor Foley for free."

The detective slipped a hand in a pants pocket and brought back another fin, folded the bill into thirds and tossed it till the coffee cup stopped it.

The *Paloma*'s First Mate unfolded his arms and leaned forward, hands on the edge of the table, but paying no apparent heed to the folded five-dollar bill. "Did you know the term 'shanghaied' started right here in this hallowed hall, Samuel Spade? Sixty-some year ago, you were showed to a den in back where the hardest liquor known to man was served, or so you be told. Then when you wake up next mornin', it's with a knockout-drop hangover on a boat sailin' the high seas, with you a loyal member of the crew."

"I wasn't buying another serving of corny local color with that fin," Spade said. "The next time I slip my hand in my pocket, it comes back with a heater in it."

Connor Foley thought about that. He leaned on his elbows.

His Long John Silver patois disappeared. "Call it another fin and we'll have a real conversation. The *Paloma*'s back in port being refitted. I'm signed on as captain but the money don't flow till then."

"Congratulations on your promotion. Negotiations will resume after I hear something from you worth another five."

The seaman's palms opened like ugly blossoms. "What can I tell you, Spade?"

"What do you know?"

Connor Foley loosened himself up with two more swigs from the coffee cup. Then he began: "We was in port, in Hong Kong, when this red-headed twist comes aboard with this big boy who looks like nobody you'd want to tangle with. They're after the captain to smuggle this object, this artifact, this statue of a black bird, into the City here. He turns 'em down at first—Jacobi got himself in Dutch smugglin' in the past and he played it straight for some time, getting his name made good again."

"He confided this in you, this transaction?"

The future captain's laugh shook the little table and the coffee cup and soda pop bottle danced. "Oh, hell no! I heard it, all of it, whole damn thing. Just happened I was accidentally right outside the captain's cabin at the time." He tugged on an ear lobe. "On a ship like the *Paloma*, best you ride the Erie."

"Not a bad policy."

The bearded man frowned, remembering. "But they put the screws to him, them two. The big guy tried to get tough, but Jacobi, he wasn't any pushover. Then the redhead came back alone and, well…she had her ways. She did have her ways. I kind of think ol' Captain Jacobi got more than just money out of that bargain."

Spade was frowning. "How much money? Never mind what the woman threw in."

The dark eyes got big under their bushy brows. "A *lot* of damn money. A goddamn fortune! When I told him what I heard, Jacobi gives me a hundred of what they give him—we're talkin' a thousand damn dollars!"

"Big money for a bird," Spade said with a straight face. The detective rose. "Don't go anywhere. I'll get us another round."

"Where have I got to go?"

Spade got a second soda pop bottle of beer and whatever the *Paloma*'s former First Mate was having in that coffee cup. He set the drinks down and himself.

"There are any number of reasons," Spade said, "why your late captain might've decided not to do business with the woman or any of that crooked crowd. But do you have any idea how your captain, with a belly full of lead, knew to bring the falcon around to my office?"

Connor Foley sipped his fresh cup and shrugged. "Probably heard your name when the *Paloma* got in port and that fat man and that redhead and that little fairy come on board."

Spade asked, "So you overheard that conversation too?"

The First Mate nodded. "Part of it. That was more than just talk…more of a ruckus where if it got any more out of hand, somebody might get themselfs shot."

"Somebody did."

The seaman, perhaps sobered by Spade's comment, took down two gulps of whatever-it-was in the coffee cup and belched loud enough to be heard over conversations, arguments, fallen bottles and breaking china, not to mention negotiations for temporary upstairs lodging with the bedraggled mermaids swimming in the Old Shipwreck café.

Spade asked, "What exactly did you overhear after you docked in San Francisco, Connor?"

"All I know is," the *Paloma* hand said, "Jacobi wanted more money from them and they didn't want to give it to him. It starts to get loud and this punk of Gutman's, the little character with the big gun, starts threatening the captain. So I get the hell away from there and into my cabin. Want no part of shooting and if the captain got himself in too deep, it's the captain who got his own damn tit in the wringer. Before long smoke starts coming from under the door and I go out in the passageway and, I'll be damned if the ship ain't on fire! I start calling out to crew but mostly just get the hell out."

"Beats being burned alive."

Connor Foley leaned forward, spoke confidentially, not difficult in the noisy "café." "Spade, do you figure Captain Jacobi had his head screwed on right?"

Spade pawed the air with a thick-fingered hand. "You knew him, I didn't. We met when he stumbled into my office and flopped down dead."

The First Mate was shaking his head. "He couldn't have been right, could he? He just couldn't!"

"Right about what?"

The future captain's dark eyes were wild. "That black bird he cut me in on for a C note. It couldn't be worth more than a gee…could it?"

The next morning, Spade caught Effie Perine out of her Mary Janes and on her tiptoes, hanging Christmas decorations on the tree in his inner office—red and green and blue and pink and yellow gleaming glass balls. The overhead light was off and both the tree and the girl glowed in the subdued light, her green dress adding a further seasonal touch. She turned to her employer as if she'd been caught with her hand in the till.

"It's Saturday, Sam," the girl said. "And you know how slow business usually is."

"Come over here and sit down," Spade said, getting behind his desk.

He had brought with him his Colt Police Positive .38 revolver, in its shoulder holster and wrapped in its attached strap. He locked these in his bottom right-hand desk drawer, not noticing how wide-eyed his secretary was seeing him with the weapon he so rarely carried.

She came over and sat, as requested, if sheepishly, bringing half a carton of the gleaming ornaments along in their cellophane and cardboard-lidded box. They rattled when she set the box down.

"I paid for those decorations myself," Effie Perine said defensively, sitting in the client's chair, putting on her shoes as primly as possible. "They're cheap—they're made in Japan."

"Never mind that," Spade said, in his swivel-chair now.

He was in the grey suit he'd worn the day Brigid O'Shaughnessy came to the office; it fit him as well as possible, considering it was off-the-rack and factoring in the broad width of his sloping shoulders and the narrowness of his waist.

The detective leaned back in his chair and got out his rolling papers and tobacco pouch from either suitcoat pocket; but then just held one each in a palm, distracted by his thoughts. With the window shut tight behind him—today was colder than it had been yet this December—the buff curtains hung limp.

His secretary half-rose from the chair, collected the cigarette makings from him, sat back down and made a roll-your-own for her boss, every bit as expert at it as he was, though she'd never smoked a day in her life.

Then Spade told her, his expression almost stupid in its blandness, his voice as uninflected as a hospital intercom announcement, what he'd learned the day before at the Old Shipwreck Café. Halfway through, he accepted the moist cylinder from her and set the tip afire with his lighter and inserted it in one side of his lips.

He concluded his monologue with a question: "Is it possible that damn dingus is nowhere in San Francisco and never has been?"

Her eyebrows rose. "It must be somewhere!"

Spade threw a hand in the air. "On God's green earth, yes. But not necessarily in San Francisco. The Russian was last known to be in London, selling a fake antiquity to the British Museum. Oh, they authenticated the statuette all right, before he pulled a switch on them, so the golden vulture does exist. It's not a pot at the end of a rainbow but very real."

Her wide-eyed expression reflected on the remaining ornaments glimmering under the cellophane in their box. "But the Russian general was in San Francisco! He died here!"

Spade sighed smoke, his eyes dreamy with thought. "He did. Kemidov got here and found Gutman and his traveling circus seeking the booty on a wild goose chase in which men were dropping dead with lead poisoning left and right. So the Russian kept undercover and let the hunt go on, since only he knew where the bird was."

She agreed: "Kept his head down."

"Till somebody caved it in for him, anyway."

Effie Perine winced at that. "What was he doing in San Francisco with the others?"

Spade tapped ash into the brass tray. "Besides avoiding them? Well, Cairo claims to know of a moneybags collector who will pay the small fortune that bird is worth. And Cairo was, and is, here in town. Under lock and key, but in town. Maybe the Russian was waiting for the dust to settle till he could get the Levantine alone."

The girl blinked at him. "At the county jail?"

Spade gestured with an open hand. "Somehow Kemidov hoped to get to Cairo. That's my guess, anyway. Posing as his lawyer, maybe—who knows? But that does indicate Kemidov likely brought the real artifact with him to San Francisco."

Her head shook and the tawny curls bounced. "But where could the dingus be, Sam?"

Hearing her call it that made him smile around the cigarette she'd made him; it bobbed as he spoke. "It's somewhere safe and out of the way—it's not something our esteemed general would carry with him. Too big for most deposit boxes, or a hotel safe—and a hotel baggage storage room wouldn't be safe enough."

The girl's brown eyes rolled. "Once one of these Gutman people knew where Kemidov was staying, they'd go straight there and burgle the place. Those storage rooms aren't even under lock and key, generally. And when they are, it just takes one little key."

Spade nodded at her wisdom. "Kemidov wanted that whole rotten bunch to think the phony bird they wound up with was the real thing, in the sense it was the actual object they'd all been chasing—that no golden jewel-feathered friend ever really existed. The Russian had several copies made to confuse the issue, to get everyone else who'd been chasing the falcon to believe he'd been running a con and throw their hands in the air, and give up the game…allowing Kemidov to raise some sucker money while he sought the big payoff."

The girl leaned her chin on her cupped hand now, arm resting on its elbow. "Courtesy of a wealthy private collector."

"Which also would've made any question of legal title a moot point, including the British Museum's fancy bill of sale. Cairo had…has…a buyer on the hook with big bucks, and Kemidov likely planned to throw in with our friend the Levantine once the others pursuing their golden goal got sidelined or exhausted or dead."

Half out of her chair, Effie Perine leaned over the desk. "But who has the falcon now, Sam?"

He gave her a single-shoulder shrug. "Maybe nobody. Maybe Kemidov died in sole possession of the knowledge of where the real *rara avis* is. If so, that knowledge died with him."

Spade's secretary frowned in thought. "So how did he get to San Francisco? Wasn't he last known to be in London? He wouldn't have left from Hong Kong like the others. Didn't he have a different ocean to cross?"

His grin turned wolfish. "You're right, sweetheart. He'd have crossed to New York by zeppelin or boat. And then by train. Possibly by air. Boeing has a service to Mills Field. More likely rail, though..."

"So they were all traveling at the same time."

"Yes, different ones of 'em by various means. Fast boat for Brigid O'Shaughnessy and Floyd Thursby, slower boat for Captain Jacobi and the object he was smuggling for them. Probably a fast boat for the fat man and Cairo and Wilmer, too, in pursuit of Brigid and Thursby and the bird. And meanwhile Kemidov and his falcon make their way here by ship and then rail or, less likely, air. Our Russian finds the Gutman circus in town. Hides the real falcon somewhere and then plays his waiting game till he can claim the thing unhindered."

She snapped her fingers, making a sharp click. "Claim it—Sam, maybe that's it. How about the baggage claims at the airport and the train station?"

Spade nodded. "Ahead of you, angel. Mills Field and Mission Street are on the docket today."

"Lots of trains from the east wind up in Oakland," she reminded him, "and the Ferry Building's the next stop for passengers, after their little boat ride."

Spade winked at her. "That's why it's my first port of call today."

He crushed out the cigarette she'd made and left it sizzling in the brass tray as he went quickly out.

CHAPTER THIRTEEN
What's in the Bag?

Spade again headed to the waterfront district, this time taking a quick taxicab to Embarcadero and Market, where the distinctive clock tower of the Beaux Arts-style Ferry Building lorded it over its two-story block-long base. At this terminal tens of thousands of daily commuters-by-ferry were accommodated while various railroads offered overland travelers buses to complete their trip to assorted accommodations in Spade's town after arriving at the Oakland terminal across the bay.

The detective, in hat but not topcoat, entered the north end of the arcade and skirted the ground-floor flower stand into a bustling world of newsboy shouts, footstep fusillades, and echoing conversation, the dissonant street music of slamming taxi doors and squealing street cars leeching into the surprisingly narrow passage between facing restaurants, newsstands and other commercial ventures. Even on a Saturday, when a rare employer gave half a day or even the full day off, the Ferry Building did not seem noticeably less crowded. The business-clad horde coming from either direction passed through an elegant but teeming two-story public area overseen by grand interior arches and sun-streaming skylights.

For all the commuter bustle, the baggage room—used by the Pacific Limited and the other lines—had no one queued up at all, and the burly middle-aged man who had lifted more than his share of heavy loads in his day regarded Spade with no apparent interest. The curator of this storehouse of checked and sometimes forgotten parcels and luggage wore a black railroad cap, a light blue work shirt and a string tie, and sported a thick black-peppered-grey mustache in a regret-grooved face.

"I wonder if you could help me," Spade said pleasantly.

"I wonder." But he didn't really.

"My wife's grandfather came out here from New York about a month ago."

"Is that so."

Spade took off his hat, as if paying respects. "We lost him recently, I'm afraid."

"Well, that is too bad."

The detective sighed, shook his head. "Stepped in front of a streetcar."

The clerk was a trifle impressed now. "Took his own life, did he?"

"Not intentionally. He was soused to the gills."

That got a smile out of the clerk, who quickly removed it and said, "Sorry, mister. No offense meant."

Spade grinned. "No, it's okay. You can laugh if you like. My wife's the one who loved the old boy. I could take him or leave him." He leaned forward confidentially. "But I have a problem."

"You do?"

The detective rested an elbow on the counter. "Gramps checked a bag here. It was too heavy for him to lug around, he said. Not in his cups when he made this deathbed observation, what was left of him anyway after the streetcar got through with him, so I'll accept it as true."

The baggage clerk seemed to be losing interest. "Have you got the claim check? It's all about the claim check."

Spade made a click in his cheek. "Wasn't among his papers, I'm afraid. The wife and me are settling up what little there is of his estate, and I could give a damn about this bag he checked. But seems he brought my wife's mother's ashes back with him."

"Oh dear," the baggage man said flatly. "Is that what's in the bag?"

Spade's face clenched. "That's what's in the bag. It's a big brass urn and likely heavy as hell. I'd hate to think what kind of official fuss might be made for you folks, what with the red tape and paperwork and all. These are human remains, after all. Well, assuming the biddy was human."

"I have a mother-in-law myself," the baggage man admitted with a quick smile that disappeared into indifference. "But you still don't have a claim check."

"That's true." Spade glanced behind him—no one was in line at the moment. The world of the Ferry Building was streaming by in its two directions, noisy and going places in both; but he and the baggage man were in their own quiet little pocket. "But I do have a name—Kemidov."

"Mister, that's—"

"And I have a double sawbuck."

The baggage man leaned out to check for more customers himself; there weren't any. "Might be able to check for you at that."

Opening a hand with a twenty-dollar bill tucked under the thumb, Spade said, "Possibility he was traveling under an assumed name. Creditors chased him out west here. So if there's nothing under Kemidov, I could toss in a fin if I could just come back there and heft any New York parcels that haven't been claimed for the last month or so."

The baggage man stroked his mustache. "Another sawbuck if you find it?"

Five minutes later, Spade left the Ferry Building with a smile and a worn black leather suitcase secured with buckled straps and tagged KEMIDOV. He took a cab back to his office building on Geary.

*

Ten minutes later Spade, in his inner office, stood at his swivel-chair behind his desk and regarded the black leather suitcase, which looked as though it might have gone through several wars. Perhaps it had.

Across from him, the client's chair pushed aside, Effie Perine stood wide-eyed, staring at the suitcase herself. Her big brown eyes held apprehension. Spade's yellow-grey ones displayed none of their casual dreaminess, instead suggested amber gemstones in a tight setting, his forehead tensed as well.

In the multi-colored glow of the Yuletide tree where the desk of Miles Archer had rested, Spade unstrapped the battered bag and tried its snaps—the valise was locked. From the pencil tray of his desk he selected a pocketknife and used its blade to pry open the bag. It took some work but finally the lid popped loose.

The detective and his secretary exchanged looks, hers anxious, his hungry.

He flipped back the lid.

Within, in a nest of crumpled newspaper, was a familiar brown paper-wrapped parcel secured with heavy twine. Leaving it within the valise, Spade turned the package, which was the size of a holiday ham, till its knot was on top. He slipped the blade of the pocketknife under the knot and paused.

"We've been here before, angel, haven't we?"

"Oh, Sam..."

His wolfish grin, however familiar, took on a wild aspect and Effie Perine shivered, seeing it.

"Shall we unwrap this under the tree?" he asked her, with quiet humor that didn't quite match his expression.

"Don't be funny, Sam," Effie Perine said, a quaver in her voice.

"Go lock up," he ordered.

She went quickly out, closing the inner office door behind her, out of habit.

Spade snapped the twine with the blade and peeled the roping off, then unwrapped the package's several layers of brown-paper skin with the excitement of a child on Christmas morning, tossing the residue to either side of the valise much as that child might do with colorful wrapping tissue getting in the way of a longed-for toy. This exposed a mass of excelsior, clinging tight to the prize but making it look plump and misshapen. This thickness of packing material Spade tore through and then peeled and tossed away the shaved wood packing fibers until a familiar shiny, coal-black surface gradually became the figure of a falcon, a foot high, which the detective removed and rested on its base.

With a sweep of his left arm, Spade scattered the packing materials, loose-strapped valise and all, onto the linoleum of the office floor, where they fell like an abrupt rain shower interrupted by one brief thunderclap.

"Angel!" Spade called. "Come see this."

Holding his pocketknife, as he stood behind his desk, Spade took the black-bird statuette into both his big hands, reacting to its heaviness, and upended it. He gripped the bird tight by its head with his left hand and carved a shaving of black from its base. One curl of black enamel was all it took.

Two colors jumped at him.

The statuette itself was golden, and winked at him as the overhead light hit it; and a single exposed jewel glowed in a partially exposed claw, red as a ruby. It almost certainly was one.

"We've got it, precious!" Spade called, an uncontrolled reaction unusual for this man. He grasped the artifact in both his thick-fingered hands, then held it against himself as if it were the Baby Jesus. "We finally caged this goddamn bird!"

He was looking toward the inner-office door when it opened and Effie Perine was framed there, her wide eyes part of an expression wholly different from that of the girl who witnessed Spade unveil the fake falcon from its brown-paper and excelsior shroud two weeks earlier.

Just behind her, as small as she was, the figure in the neat grey cap—his face expressionless save for sad long-lashed eyes and a small wound of a thin-lipped smile—held an automatic pistol against one side of the secretary's pale white throat, the weapon's blunt nose dimpling the surrounding flesh.

"Been watching us, have you, son?" Spade said, as if welcoming a relative to a holiday get-together.

"Crack wise and see where it gets you," the boy with the automatic pistol said. "And her."

Wilmer Cook's little-boy face was badly bruised, a display of orange and red and black, alongside his left cheek where Spade had kicked him not long ago. The detective knew the punk had in the past carried two of those pistols in the oversize topcoat that made him seem as small as the pistol in Effie Perine's neck made him seem big, in terms of threat at least, with the possibility of the other gun being pressed against the secretary's back a near certainty.

The boy walked Effie Perine slowly in, blocked almost entirely by her, stopping a few steps inside Spade's inner chamber.

"Nobody has to die here today," Spade said serious but unthreatening, still on his feet behind his desk with the Maltese falcon in his thick-fingered grasp. "We gave each other as good as we got last time, and maybe we can let it go at that."

"Maybe," Wilmer Cook said. He smiled a little and it was no improvement on his rosy-cheeked, pasty, partly bruised face. "Start with handing over the bird."

Spade shifted the heavy object into his right hand, taking it by the middle, barely able to get his fingers around it. He held it out.

"You can have the goddamn thing," Spade said. "Let the girl go and come get it. You've got the guns. I'm not packing. You know I don't like the damn things."

Wilmer Cook thought about it.

Effie Perine stomped on the boy's right foot and ducked to her left. The boy still had the pistol in his right hand aimed in the general direction of the girl's neck, but the gun in the gunsel's left hand was exposed now, as was he, at least enough so for Spade to fling the falcon at the intruder with all the power he could muster. The black-enameled golden bird flew like a football from an expert quarterback and caught Wilmer Cook in the forehead with a crack so loud it might have been a gunshot.

But no gun had been fired, not either of the ones in the boy's hands, as the priceless artifact clunked to the floor like the blunt object it had become. Effie Perine had slipped further away from her captor, and now turned, aghast if relieved to see scarlet blood streaming down the young face between startled eyes as the slight figure in the grey cap and oversize topcoat tottered on feet no longer receiving signals.

Like a felled pine, Wilmer Cook collapsed forward, a gun in either limp hand, barely so. One big automatic pistol under unfeeling fingers seemed to point to the black falcon, with the intruder on his face and the bird on its back, as if a hunter had bagged it on the fly.

Effie Perine stood with a small pink-nailed hand over her mouth to stifle a scream that never came, and Spade got to her just as she turned away from the corpse and came into his arms. He soothed her, patted her back, said, "Good girl, good girl."

"Oh, Sam. Oh, Sam. What now?"

He walked her toward the door between the inner and outer offices. "Go back to your desk and wait. You don't need to be in here looking at that." He indicated the dead Wilmer Cook with a half-glance. "You have to stick around, though. You're a witness."

"I'm not going anywhere," Effie Perine said softly. "It isn't five o'clock."

Spade laughed. "No, it isn't. Pour yourself a cup of coffee from that thermos of yours. I'll call Tom Polhaus and get the coppers over here."

Effie Perine glanced behind her as she and her boss went through. She seemed to be looking at Wilmer Cook, but she said, "What about that? The falcon? It's real, isn't it?"

The place where Spade had peeled off some of the black enamel was gleaming, gold and red.

"This time," he said, "it's real."

In the company of Wilmer Cook's sprawled corpse, and with the coppery scent of blood in his nostrils, Spade at his desk got on the phone and directed the operator to put him through to Davenport 2-0-2-0, Detective Bureau.

Sergeant Tom Polhaus answered.

Spade told his friend everything that had happened. Along the way, Tom made appropriate one-syllable expressions of interest and surprise.

When Spade had finished, Tom sighed. "So it's the real megillah this time, this falcon."

"Jen-you-wine."

"I'll get the morgue wagon over there," Tom said. "And I'll be over myself after I round the Lieutenant up. He'll want to be in on this."

Spade grinned at the receiver. "I'm sure Dundy will thank me for wrapping up another case for him."

"Yeah. You can expect him to bring a bottle of bubbly along." Tom's voice shifted from friendship mode to business. "Listen, your office is a crime scene now. Don't touch anything."

"You may find my fingerprints here and there."

"Don't rub it in, Sam. There are procedures. Like we'll have to take photographs…and of course take that bird into evidence."

"Sure," Spade said affably. "But I'll want it back. Possession is nine-tenths of the law, I hear."

"But we'll have possession."

"After you sign for it. No, the chain of title on this baby is complicated. And I have things to sort out with assorted clients."

"Speaking of which…" Tom paused, possibly weighing his words. When he continued, he was almost whispering. "I have some information for you that I ain't supposed to share just yet."

"The best kind. Give."

The police detective sighed again. "We've mounted a thorough background check on the late Casper Gutman, at the request of District Attorney Bryan. Turns out your fat friend never had no daughter. Or son, or wife either, for that matter."

Spade winced but kept it out of his voice. "What about a bastard child here or there?"

"That's always a possibility, but nothing turns up with the cops in New York, which is where he was mostly from, and the D.C. boys don't have any offspring on file for him either, and they have quite a packet on the fat man. Him having a daughter that slipped through the cracks is pretty unlikely, no matter what name she was registered under at the Alexandria—and while Gutman engaged in perverse activities, his tastes didn't run to girls, if you catch my drift. That Wilmer was his gunsel in more ways than one. Gunsel's Yiddish for kept boy, you know."

"You don't say."

"So if this Rhea Gutman is a client, be that as it may. Keep in mind she may be an accomplice in Gutman's crowd—but as a daughter? She's strictly a phony."

Spade thought about that. "Appreciate the info, Tom. Wilmer Cook and I will be waiting here for you and your charming superior officer. Effie's a witness, so bring a notebook."

They rang off.

Without a glance at either the dead man or the black bird on its back, beak up, Spade went out into the reception office. He poured and drank a cup coffee from the thermos on Effie Perine's desk. She looked up at him.

He answered her unspoken question. "The representatives of law and order are on their way," he told her. Then almost to himself, he said: "Somebody was betting on me having a guilty conscience."

"A long shot if I ever heard of one," Effie Perine said. Then she thought about it. "Why do you say that, Sam?"

"Just a notion I've got," Spade said.

CHAPTER FOURTEEN
Christmas Party

Spade entered his office from the outer one, leaving the connecting door slightly ajar, then welcomed with open arms the four clients who'd assembled at the far right of his inner sanctum, where these apparent strangers stood loosely grouped in shared bewilderment.

Each guest had been telephoned earlier in the day by Effie Perine with an invitation to an informal holiday-season get-together of Spade agency clients at seven that Sunday evening. She had urged each to attend at Mr. Spade's personal request —he had important news to share, new information specific to each.

His guests had arrived more or less on time, within minutes of one other. As a group, they had chatted somewhat awkwardly, milling in the area where, unbeknownst to them, the bodily remains of Wilmer Cook had sprawled the day before, waiting for collection.

"Greetings everyone," Spade said, as he positioned himself behind his desk, then remained standing while he made the introductions.

"Mr. Monahan is in the gaming business in Chicago," Spade said jovially. "Dixie, welcome."

In formal wear with a black bow tie and high collar, the gambler gave his fellow guests an embarrassed wave.

"Miss Wonderly," Spade said, indicating the girl, "is Brigid O'Shaughnessy's sister and hails from New York. Thank you for coming, Corrine."

Her Clara Bow figure fetchingly apparent in her short pink-tiered velvet dress with matching clutch purse, the auburn-haired beauty smiled nervously at the three other guests.

"Steward Blackwood is visiting us all the way from London," Spade said, "where he is quite the important figure with the British Museum."

In a vested grey herringbone suit, the distinguished curator lifted his silver-handled, black-stemmed walking stick in waist-high salute.

"And Rhea Gutman," Spade said rather more seriously of this final guest of the four, "is the daughter of the late Casper Gutman. I'm sure we all wish you our condolences on your father's recent passing, Miss Gutman."

The fair-haired, red-cheeked young woman, petite in a lightweight grey suit with grey felt hat, a black-and-silver handbag on a strap over a shoulder, tilted her head and smiled, in acknowledgment.

"Now if you'll help yourself to refreshment," Spade said, "and can get yourself into the holiday spirit, I'll give all of you my proper holiday wishes."

Other than Effie Perine's dressy white-collared green frock, the only evidence of this being a Christmas party was the well-trimmed evergreen with its tinsel and colorful glowing electric bulbs to Spade's right, opposite the area to his left with its maple card table on which rested a big cream-colored, gilt-edged punch bowl sporting "Tom & Jerry" in gold letters, with half a dozen matching cup-like mugs forming a crescent around it. The hostess herself had brought the set from home while Spade provided the necessary rum and cognac for the nutmeg-batter recipe.

The private detective's secretary served cups of punch on paper napkins to the confused guests, who exchanged wary smiles and pleasantries until she directed them toward the desk of their host, whose motive for the punch was to keep the hands of the attendees occupied.

Now here they were, all seated across from the detective at his desk in wooden folding chairs and holding cups of punch and napkins somewhat awkwardly, occasionally trading uncomfortable glances. The chamber's overhead lighting was off, a few table lamps spotted here and there on this file cabinet and that credenza providing pockets of illumination, as did the tied-back window curtains letting in the city at night in all its firefly flickering.

"If you are wondering where the rest of my clients are this evening," Spade said affably, "this gathering is strictly for you four who've each given me a retainer to find the Maltese falcon."

The two men reacted as if receiving a slap while the two women shared a frowning intake of breath.

Dixie Monahan leaned forward in his chair, his skimpy mustache twitching in irritation. "What the hell's the idea of bringing the lot of us together? How is that in any way ethical?"

"Ethics take a back seat," Spade said, "when people start dying violently around you."

The red of Rhea Gutman's cheeks now spread to her entire heart-shaped face. "What kind of detective are you, anyway, Mister Spade? Bilking the four of us when we each have the same goal?"

"I haven't bilked anybody," Spade said. "I took on no client whose interests were in conflict with any other's."

Dixie Monahan said, "That's nonsense! I'll have my money back or have you put up on charges."

Spade began to roll a cigarette, methodical yet casual, as if he were seated here alone. "Seeing a Chicago boy like you go to the cops for aid and comfort, Monahan, might be damned entertaining."

Corrine Wonderly, anger tightening her voice, said, "I offered you a five-hundred dollar retainer, you awful man. But you just sent me away!"

"You offered me more than that," Spade said rudely, as he lighted the smoke, then snapped shut his lighter.

The Wonderly girl huffed indignantly but Spade just smiled.

Steward Blackwood leaned on his walking stick, saying, "Must I remind you, sir, that if and when you do find the missing artifact, I represent a venerable institution with an unquestionably valid chain of title? And that you were paid a five-hundred-dollar retainer for locating the item, against much more?"

"A non-refundable retainer," Spade reminded him, gesturing with the cigarette in hand, held between fore- and middle finger.

From her punch-bowl station, Effie Perine watched, hands clasped before her, taking in the boss in action. Her expression might have indicated pride or excitement, possibly both.

"You were promised new information," Spade told the group, issuing the statement in a wreath of tobacco smoke. "We'll start with Wilmer Cook—your father's friend, Rhea."

"He's no friend of mine," she snapped.

"He's nobody's friend now," he said. "He died in this office, not long ago."

Gasps came from the women and the mouths of the two men dropped open like trapdoors.

"Right over there," Spade said, nodding toward where they'd milled and sipped punch. "This new linoleum flooring made clean-up a cinch."

Dixie Monahan said, "Someone was killed in here? What in Christ's name is this all about, Spade?"

"Good to hear you honoring the birthday we're about to celebrate," Spade said with his wolfish grin. "The punk barged in here holding that sweet young woman hostage…" He indicated Effie Perine at her punch bowl. "…with a gun at her neck and another in her back. She managed to slip free and I hurled something solid at him, caught him right in the head and shut his lights off. He went down hard and stayed down."

Dixie Monahan looked pale; the two women appeared alarmed, although the British Museum man did not seem terribly impressed, resting a hand on his stick.

The Chicago gambler asked: "Do the police know?"

"This was yesterday," Spade said, as if discussing ancient history, "and they came and collected him. Or I should say the morgue wagon did. The object I threw at the gunsel, cracking his thin skull, they were good enough to leave behind. They didn't need it as evidence in what was obviously a self-defense situation. The object, by the way, is right over there, under the tree. Tucked back, but if you look good and hard, you can make it out."

Four heads turned toward Effie Perine's glittering Christmas tree, the glass balls among the tinsel and electric bulbs reflecting the lights colorfully. Standing on its base, but snugged back a bit, and partially concealed by the white plush gold-sequined cotton Christmas tree skirt, and with Wilmer Cook's blood cleaned off, stood the black-enameled bird.

"It's…" the Wonderly girl began.

"…the falcon," Rhea Gutman finished.

The women were craning their necks toward the tree and the ebony "gift" under it. Both men were on their feet, also with their eyes on the statue perched there.

"Sit down," Spade said sternly. "Both of you. Everybody settle."

They did, in muttering shock.

Dixie Monahan's features clenched. "What is this, Spade? A goddamn auction?"

"No," Spade said. "There are two possibly legal claims that I know of for this *rara avis*, and two of you are the claimants. One is Casper Gutman's daughter, Rhea, who tells me she has a signed bill of sale tucked away in the Alexandria Hotel safe. And Mr. Steward Blackwood of the British Museum has the other, which I have a copy of."

The museum man and Rhea Gutman locked eyes. Corrine Wonderly was frowning, perhaps frightened, while the Chicago gambler wore the expression of a rejected suitor, clearly aware he was out of the running.

Spade's attention went to Rhea Gutman. "I don't suppose you brought that bill of sale along. Or a reasonable facsimile thereof?"

"No," she said.

"Maybe you could share the date on that document," Spade said. "Just until we can actually see it."

"I don't think so," she said stubbornly.

"My assumption," the private detective said, "is that the courts will uphold the earlier date between the British museum and yours. If your bill of sale truly exists. Of course, we can't know if Kemidov sold anyone else the dingus and pulled what may have been a usual switch for him—show the mark the real jeweled golden paperweight, then deliver a black-enameled fake. We know several, at least, were made. And we can't ask him and find out, not that he'd tell us the truth anyway."

His expression sour, Dixie Monahan said disgustedly, "You never did find the Russian, did you, Spade? Since that's all I hired you for, maybe you'd be good enough to refund *my* retainer."

Spade blew out a stream of smoke. "Oh, I found him, all right."

The gambler sat up as did the two women, though the museum man seemed almost bored, leaning on his walking stick, perhaps confident that his claim was the overruling one.

"Ran into him myself," Spade said.

"If you found him," Steward Blackwood said, "why isn't he here with us today? General Kemidov's certainly a key figure in all this, and at the very least an interested party, even having sold off the statue."

Spade's sloping shoulders rose and fell. "Well, he couldn't make the guest list—he had somewhere else to be."

"And where is that?"

"A morgue tray. I saw him on one a few nights ago."

That brought an exclamation of horror from Rhea Gutman and an unbelieving laugh from the gambler.

The museum man, his tone bordering on amusement, said, "So now he's just another one of those people dying violently around you. You seem to be a plague carrier, sir."

Spade put out his cigarette. "It's getting to be a long list, I grant you, if you add Kemidov to it. Miles Archer, Floyd Thursby, Captain Jacobi, Casper Gutman, and now Wilmer Cook. Before long, Brigid O'Shaughnessy might be added to that inventory, if the hangman has his way.... Oh, Miss Wonderly, forgive me. That was unthinking of me."

"It's all right," said the girl in the pink party dress.

Spade grinned, shook his head. "She's pretty good at landing on her feet, your sister. I told Brigid when I sent her over to the cops that with her looks and a male jury, she can probably get a life sentence and be out in twenty years, still a relatively young woman."

Corrine Wonderly said nothing, her face a blank slate.

"Thing is," Spade said, and his tone seemed almost melancholy, "you're not too upset about it, are you? Because you're not Corrine Wonderly. Who are you, really?"

The big light-blue eyes grew bigger. "Are you insane?"

"Well, it doesn't matter what your name is, in a way. I have a pretty good idea who you are." He wagged a forefinger at her. "Renting the room at the Coronet where your 'sister' stayed, that was a good touch. Was it your idea? Or Kemidov's?"

The other three had their eyes on her now, their expressions astonished.

The auburn-haired girl reacted sullenly, folding her arms to her ripe bosom. "I don't know what you're talking about."

"You don't look at all like your 'sister'—I noticed that from the start. I figure you for Kemidov's mistress. Or maybe you prefer 'girlfriend'—hell, you might even be his wife. It's unlikely you're just some twist on the game or running a con who Kemidov stumbled onto. You'd need to be more seasoned than that. Either a seasoned accomplice or his bed partner or, hell, both."

Her nostrils flared. "None of that is true. None of it!"

Spade gestured with an open hand. "This is Sunday and we're enjoying a little holiday soiree. But Monday will be here before you know it, and I'll be able to find a few things out. Maybe it'll take involving the cops, maybe not. But among the things easily confirmed is that you must have specifically asked to rent the room your 'sister' had, to better play me for a sucker. You may have fingerprints that can be traced and a whole rap sheet may well turn up, soon enough, if you're an American. Maybe you're just another one of these grifters working Europe, like Casper Gutman and his crowd—only it's not Gutman's crowd you're part of, is it? If you're really just Kemidov's moll, the feds can get that from their overseas equivalents. Might take some time, so you may be able to take a run-out powder before anything hits the fan. I won't try to stop you."

Perched on the edge of her chair, the false Corrine Wonderly turned to her left and right, pleading her case as if to a jury: "It's none of it true! None of it, I swear."

Spade's laugh was a harsh thing. "Don't waste your breath, honey. The fun part is yet to come." He spoke to the others, moving face to face. "You know how I knew that stiff in the morgue was Kemidov? I identified him thanks to one thing..." His dreamy yellow-grey eyes returned to the auburn-haired girl. "...a photo of him taken with your 'sister' Brigid. That you gave to me. Only it wasn't Kemidov, was it? The man in that photo, the man on that morgue slab, just about has to be the real Steward Blackwood. How he and Brigid wound up in the same photo I can't tell you. Or exactly how a museum curator wound up in the county jail ice box. But I figure the late Steward Blackwood was on the trail of the falcon himself, not as a venal collector but a representative of the British Museum, and I would bet every cent of the retainer given me by the fake Blackwood that the real one had wrapped up legal ownership of that damned bird of prey."

The ersatz Steward Blackwood flew to his feet. In the grasp of his right hand was the silver handle of the walking stick, which when removed became a handgun, its eye trained on Spade as was every other eye in the room.

Spade rose slowly, hands up at his waist, palms out. "You met with him, didn't you, General Kemidov? Right here in the States where Blackwood did his research into colonial knick-knacks. Signed the falcon over to him, legally. And when things started to go bad, with the Gutman bunch closing in, and Blackwood handy, you bashed his brains in. From behind, of course. And took the legal agreement with you, to use on suckers like me until the time came to destroy it, to provide the world with a dead Russian general and give yourself the identity of a British Museum mucky-muck, so you could pocket the British payoff and sell the falcon all over again...maybe to this rich collector Joel Cairo has on the line."

"Collect it, Felice," Kemidov said to the fake Corrine, his eyes and his silver gun on Spade, but his head nodding toward the decorated pine tree and the gift under it.

The girl in the pink dress scurried to the glowing tree, where she knelt like a child Christmas morning and grabbed up the falcon. The exposed ruby in its base winked at their audience.

"It's heavy," Felice grunted, struggling with it in a two-armed grasp.

Spade said, "That's the weight of too many dead men."

To Kemidov's right, Monahan had moved away a few steps, while to the General's left, Rhea Gutman backed off a few feet. Both did so slowly, making no sudden moves.

The Russian kicked away the wooden folding chair he'd been seated in and it went rattling off to one side. "Keep those hands up, Spade," the English accent replaced by a softly Russian one. "Keep them up."

Then Kemidov's mistress, with the bird clutched to her bosom as if she were its mother, arrived at his side and they backed away from Spade at his desk and the other two guests at either end of the lined-up chairs, Monahan exuding rage and resentment while Rhea Gutman appeared afraid.

Neither the General nor his mistress heard Sergeant Tom Polhaus come up behind him. Tom looped an arm around the man's neck and another around his middle, squeezing tight, the little silver gun tumbling from the Russian's fingers and clattering to the floor. Moving more slowly, Lieutenant Dundy held his outstretched hands out to the mistress, who wincingly passed him the Maltese falcon.

Spade came out from behind his desk and found Effie Perine at his side.

The General's woman looked at Spade hatefully and spoke two words.

"She's upset," the secretary observed.

The detective said, "Maybe she's Wilmer Cook's sister."

CHAPTER FIFTEEN
A Different Path

Tom Polhaus and Lieutenant Dundy didn't stay at the party long. They had caught the male perpetrator and his female accomplice in the armed-robbery act and would drag them off to County Jail #1 to join Joel Cairo and Brigid O'Shaughnessy, the cast of incarcerated characters in the Maltese falcon saga growing.

On his way out, taking a scowling Kemidov by the arm, the ruddy-faced Tom said, "We'll leave the swag to you, this time, Sam. Dundy says if we need the statuette for the trial, we'll be in touch."

Spade nodded toward Dundy, leading the fake Corrine Wonderly out by the arm.

Spade grunted a laugh. "Your lieutenant hates to thank me for anything, doesn't he?"

"He clocked you last time," Tom said, looking back with a shrug, hauling the Russian, "you clocked him this time. Maybe you two can call it even and get on with your lives. Some people just rub each other the wrong way."

Then Polhaus, the Russian, Lt. Dundy and the Russian's moll were just footsteps echoing away in the corridor.

Dixie Monahan, looking like a fancy restaurant's waiter in his tux, took his leave shortly thereafter, telling Spade, "If you wind up with that bastard of a bird, let me know. I'll get us a buyer."

"I'll keep that in mind," Spade said.

The departing guest raised his eyebrows and put them back

down. "If any tough babies from Chicago come around looking for me, you ain't seen me."

"Dixie who?"

The two men exchanged grins and shook hands, and the gambler was gone.

Effie Perine—after switching on the overhead light and conducting a little clean-up of the Tom & Jerry serving table—unplugged the electric lights on the Christmas tree and asked her boss if it was all right to wait till Monday morning to tidy up after the inner-office party.

Spade said, "Good idea, but I'm only going to work you till noon, precious. It'll be Christmas Eve, after all. And I'm no Ebenezer Scrooge."

"Ah, you're sweet, Sam," she said and took his right hand and squeezed it in hers.

"Yeah, I get that all the time."

He gave her a whispered goodbye and she smiled and nodded and went out. The detective closed the connecting door but not before the sound of the outer one onto the corridor shutting announced his secretary's departure.

Seated in the one remaining wooden folding chair—Spade had reflexively folded the rest up and put them away in the inner-office closet—was the last of the clients at his Christmas party, the petite and pretty Rhea Gutman. She sat watching him patiently putting the chairs away, picture perfect in her grey hat and dress, the little beaded black-and-silver bag in her lap.

He walked over and gave her a smile. "I hoped you might linger."

Mid-desk nearby, the black statuette perched regally on its base opposite the young woman.

"What's to become of that?" Rhea Gutman asked, with a nod

toward the object, as if asking where the punch bowl might be stored.

Spade sat nearby on the edge of his desk next to the black-enameled bird, folded his arms, grinned at her, with for once nothing wolfish about it.

"Remains to be seen," he said. "I intend to put the dingus in an oversize safe deposit box at Pacific States Savings and Loan until my lawyer can sort out who owns the thing."

Gutman's daughter frowned a little. "Doesn't it belong to the British Museum?"

"Doubtful." The private detective got out his tobacco pouch and papers, and began to roll a cigarette, in no hurry about it. "They paid off a con man, the alive-and-well General Kemidov, and he delivered them a statue all right, just not one worth much more than a shooting-gallery prize made of plaster. Of course, there was enough shooting in this affair to rate a special prize."

She cocked her head; twin sleek blonde arcs peeked out from either side of her grey hat. "If the museum doesn't have ownership, who does?"

He licked the cigarette shut. "Probably me. Possession being nine-tenths of the law and all."

The big golden brown eyes regarded him unblinkingly. "Am I still your client?"

"Well, of course you are."

She cocked her head and raised an eyebrow. "And didn't I pay you a thousand dollars to find and deliver the falcon? And didn't you ask, and receive, three hundred more?"

Spade fired up the roll-your-own. "That's a very good point, Rhea. Of course you promised I'd be a full partner if I found it and turned it over to you, but that's out, now. But I am willing to refund your retainer."

"I thought we were partners in this."

He sighed smoke. "Maybe you can convince me to stay partnered up—we could cut Joel Cairo in, if he hooks us up with a wealthy buyer. Do you think if your father were here he'd approve of that? That at least his daughter would see something from the seventeen years he put into the hunt, not to mention getting shot and killed over the thing."

Her reply came matter of fact: "You can be very cruel, can't you, Mr. Spade?"

Now his smile did turn wolfish. "So we're back to 'Mr. Spade' again. You can be cruel, too, darling. Maybe that's what we see in each other."

Her white-gloved hand came up from her lap and a little black automatic pistol, a .25 caliber Colt, seemed to point itself at him. Spade and the Maltese falcon were still perched on the desk, side by side, his arms remaining folded, cigarette dangling from his lips. He wore that familiar dreamy expression and seemed utterly unconcerned.

The girl's golden-brown eyes were hooded and her full lips smiled slightly, bright red against the paleness of her heart-shaped face.

"Is that what you think I'm all about?" she asked, and a faint hurt colored her voice. "That stupid black bird? And the money it might bring? Or maybe you think I want revenge for my father's murder. Didn't you give me that already, when you made a weapon out of that horrible statue, and took poor sad little Wilmer's life? Right over there it was, you said."

With her free hand she gestured to where Wilmer had fallen. But then she raised the little pistol and it pointed right at his chest.

"I recommend a head shot," Spade said, gesturing with the cigarette in hand. "You'd have to hit my heart to kill me with a bullet to the body. And you wouldn't want to have to deal with a wounded animal, would you? They can be vicious, fighting for their life."

Her eyes tensed. "You're not afraid?"

Spade took tobacco smoke in and let it out, then stared at her through the drifting grey haze it made. "Not just yet, no."

Her chin came up; its tremble was barely visible but Spade saw it easily enough. She said, "Why, might I ask?"

His shrug could not have been more casual. "You're not through gloating. But that's only because you think I don't know who you really are…though I've suspected long enough."

She frowned, swallowed, then put her red smile back on. "And who am I?"

He pointed the cigarette at her, as if it and her purse gun were about to exchange fire. "You're Brigid O'Shaughnessy's sister. The real Corrine Wonderly."

Her eyes widened, whites showing all around.

Out the window behind Spade, the city made traffic sounds and glimmered in the darkness like the black bird if its jewels were exposed.

"Don't care to try denying it?" he asked.

Her eyes glistened with tears but the gun stayed steady in her white-gloved grasp.

Casually, occasionally taking in and letting out smoke, he said, "There never was a Rhea Gutman, was there? No daughter whose fat father brought innocent her into his corrupt life. It was you who traveled, at least for a time, with your sister and the Gutman gang, which is what they were—a gang of grifters and con men and thieves, seekers of fabulous fortunes they never had to earn or even inherit. My bet is you came from an impoverished background, parents dead maybe, or just lowlife people you two good-looking girls wanted to get away from as soon as possible."

The red lips were noticeably trembling. "Why would I pretend to be Gutman's daughter?"

He pointed with the cigarette. "Because, in that company, it made it easier for Gutman to hand you off to the various men you were sent to charm and—not meaning to offend you, since that *is* a gun you're holding—occasionally seduce."

"I never slept with any of them," she said with wounded dignity, apparently not realizing the confession she had just made as to her real identity.

"You did once," Spade said softly, with a certain sadness, "that I know of."

She bolted to her feet. "You are a terrible man."

With his hands raised, palms out, the cigarette dangling, he slipped down off the desk and faced her while the falcon watched expressionlessly.

"Before you go squeezing that trigger," he said, nodding at the pistol, "there's something you might keep in mind. You're the only one in this farce besides myself who hasn't committed an actual crime—oh, I killed Wilmer all right, but it was obvious self-defense. Not even Lt. Dundy would try to prove otherwise. All you ever did, that I know of, was assume a false identity, which is a misdemeanor at worst. I figure you were on the con because your sister dragged you in. Weeks ago, when this mess first came to a head, we did our dance, you and I, in the Alexandria Hotel suite—with you willingly doped by Gutman just enough to be credible in requiring a Good Samaritan like me to help you walk it off."

Her voice, steady till now, quavered. "What…what choice did I have?"

"Probably not much. Playing the ingenue in one sting or another was your job, as the fat man's unlikely beauty of a daughter. But then things got out of hand, and you found yourself tied up with outright theft and bloody murder. I'm guessing all of that's more than you bargained for. Yet you stayed involved."

Her expression was defensively defiant. "Somebody had to look out for Brigid. You certainly didn't. That's why you're on the wrong side of this gun, Samuel Spade."

His eyes had lost their dreaminess. "If all this was about was killing me, you've had plenty of chances. Why didn't you?"

She was shaking now, not much, but visibly so. And the little .25 remained steady enough. "I...I didn't count on feeling anything about you but anger. I didn't count on feeling anything for you but resentment...for you turning my sister over to... to..."

"Justice?"

Taking a step closer to her, Spade said, "You came to me at your sister's jailhouse urging—even now she's thirsting for the falcon fortune, and maybe my hide. That's why Brigid encouraged me to help 'Rhea Gutman.' Well, she has her way of looking at the world. Do you share it? Shoot me and you'll be moving into the cell next door to her. Hand me that gun and you can walk out of here and make a clean start. You might even consider heading down a path your sister didn't take. Or is getting a share of the falcon loot all you really care about, too?"

That made her flinch. "Isn't...isn't that what you really care about?"

"I'm not in business for my health. What's the goddamn Maltese falcon to me but just another job?"

He was closer yet to her now. His hands went to her waist, firm but gentle. Between was just enough space for her little fist and the little gun in it.

Spade drew her to him, the nose of the .25 nudging him as he kissed her, tenderly at first, then almost savagely. After their lips parted, she stayed in his arms, close enough for a second kiss. The nose of the weapon poked deeper into his belly.

"How did you know?" she asked, drawing away slightly, trembling. "How long have you known?"

"Almost from the start. Remember that story I told you, about the writer who went to Hollywood? The price he paid for being part of a long-ago murder? Even changing his name didn't change that. He wound up killing himself. Kill me, Corrine, and you kill yourself."

Her eyes were tight, tears brimming. "You didn't answer how you knew…or anyway why you suspected."

It took him a while to answer. "You reminded me of her. Of…your sister. Kemidov's girlfriend had the name but not… not anything else, really."

Love and hate fought for her expression. "I should squeeze this trigger."

Spade swallowed thickly. "Maybe you should. But is it worth throwing your life away?"

They stood together in an embrace as terrible as it was wonderful, for seconds that might have been hours.

Then Corrine Wonderly, the real Corrine, reached past Spade and put the gun on his desk next to the black-enameled bird, the clunk echoing. She studied his face and then she placed her right hand against his left cheek and kissed him again. Just a tender little kiss that didn't go anywhere but away with her when she fled his arms and his office, and his world.

Spade watched her rush through the outer office and through the door, into the corridor, closing him off behind her.

Effie Perine stepped into Spade's inner office with her own small weapon in hand, a .22 revolver, and stood almost as close to him as Brigid O'Shaughnessy's sister had. She looked up at him with worry that was just starting to fade.

She said, "That's a relief. Gone and good riddance. Some of the things you said to her—were you trying to get yourself killed?" She shuddered. "I was afraid I wouldn't be able to help after all, as close as she was to you."

"She was," Spade admitted. "Too close."

CHAPTER SIXTEEN
The Return

In a wooden booth at the St. Mark's fountain and café, Spade bought Tom Polhaus breakfast. As they ate their bacon and eggs, occasionally sipping black coffee, the barrel-bellied, carelessly shaven cop, whose small dark eyes held a shrewdness many missed, mopped up egg yolk with the remains of a golden slice of toast.

Tom said, "We booked Kemidov and his moll on armed robbery while we're investigating the murder of the real Steward Blackwood."

Spade drank coffee, then said, "Considering the value of what the Russian tried to steal, you might bump that to grand larceny. But who am I to tell you boys how to do your business?"

"That ain't funny, Sam," Tom said. "Anyway, it's D.A. Bryan's call not ours."

The police detective nodded to the newspaper-and-twine-wrapped package to his right that rested vertically between them, bumping a napkin holder. He said, "I don't suppose that's a loaf of bread."

"No, that's the dingus all right," Spade said. "My next stop is the bank to rent a nice big deposit box to stuff it in. Then it's off to Samuels Jewelers to pick Effie up a Christmas present."

"Careful what you buy her, Sam," Tom said with one half of a smile and one wooly raised eyebrow. "The message you send matters."

"Ah, I'm through with women."

Tom nibbled the yellow-soaked toast. "Sure you are."

✲

"It's lovely, Sam," Effie Perine said, eyes filled with the wristwatch in the gift box she'd just divested of its sky-blue wrapping paper. She was sitting at the foot of the office Christmas tree, beaming in its glow, and Spade was nearby, on his haunches.

The delicate timepiece in its elegant case featured a face with green and white enamel zigzag and triangular patterns.

"It's fourteen karat gold-fill-on-brass," Spade said, repeating what the gaunt clerk had told him.

"Like your falcon," she said, buckling on the watch.

"Like both of the birds," Spade said. "Only those were enamel-fill—over un-precious metal last time, and the one I tucked away at the bank this morning is gold."

She took time out from admiring the Elgin on her wrist to look at her boss and say, "Open yours, Sam."

Spade tore off the brown-and-white masculine paper on a box about the size of a chocolate sampler. But candy was not what it held: a burnished brown tobacco pipe with a curved stem nestled in tissue paper next to a small round tin of pipe tobacco and a book.

"It's a Dunhill," she said of the pipe. "From England. A little like Sherlock Holmes smokes but not so bulky. I know how you like to sit on your couch and puff away and read in the evening. Take a look at the book."

On the dust-wrapper was a cameo silhouette of Holmes in his familiar deerstalker cap, smoking a similarly shaped pipe, the book's title and author in black and the background pink.

"*The Case Book of Sherlock Holmes*," Spade said, pleased. "This is the new one, isn't it? Maybe I can pick up a few tips."

With a smile, she said, "Always good to know what the competition is up to."

They stood and she kissed his cheek, just a peck.

They were standing close when she said, reluctantly, "Now you're not going to like me as much."

"Oh? Why's that?"

She stepped away. "I'm the bearer of bad news. Iva Archer is going to stop by some time before we close up shop at noon."

He shuddered. "I don't suppose I can just slip away."

She was at the open connecting door between inner and outer offices. "Don't be such a coward."

And Effie Perine went through and got behind her desk.

Spade got behind his, taking the pipe and the book with him. But the pipe was for later. For now he rolled a cigarette.

Iva Archer came in wearing a forced smile and a festive red seersucker dress with a matching cloche hat, her blonde hair peek-a-booing out. Her make-up may have been overdone but she was nonetheless a lovely woman of thirty-some with well-modeled, admirable curves.

"I wanted to stop by, Sam," Iva Archer said, as she crossed the room to where he sat at his desk smoking sullenly, "and wish you, genuinely wish you, a happy Christmas."

"Well, I genuinely wish you one, too." The V of his eyebrows flattened into a straight line. "Not wearing widow's weeds anymore, I see."

"No," she said, and sighed. "I paid Miles his due respect. I don't want to be too ridiculous a hypocrite. You know how I came to detest him."

"I remember." He breathed out smoke and sat up. "Was there something particular you wanted? We didn't really leave the door open for social calls."

The widow Archer eased down into the client's chair; she held a red-beaded clutch purse in her lap as she perched there primly, knees together beneath the textured red fabric. "I didn't like the way we left things. I just couldn't leave them there."

"We left them about where they needed to be."

Iva sat forward, eyes wide, mouth red and moist, painfully,

almost believably earnest. "Sam, you were my late husband's partner and there are business concerns that will associate us, at least in the near future, until things are settled."

He tapped cigarette ashes into the brass tray. "The contract between Miles and me was straightforward, Iva. There really isn't much of anything to settle."

Her expression became hurt. "There's…the personal side."

Spade said nothing, turning his head as he expelled smoke, politely keeping it away from his holiday visitor.

The attractive woman sat back, clutching the clutch purse. "I thought you should know…I'm moving to Oakland."

"All the way to Oakland, huh?"

Iva frowned, hurt further. "Don't be mean, Sam. I'm taking a little apartment near Phil, and when enough time has passed, we'll tie the knot and I'll move into his place with him."

"Well, that's where you'll find him."

Her laugh was more forced than her smile had been. "This must be a great weight off your mind, having me out of your life. Pestering you. Reminding you of…things."

"I wish you well, Iva," he said, doing the best he could with the words.

She swallowed, her manner hesitant now. "Phil…Phil asked me to tell you something."

Spade gestured toward the outer office. "Oh, he didn't come along? Isn't he waiting in the hall?"

"I asked you not to be mean." She drew in a breath. "He's terribly embarrassed about the way he behaved and wants you to know there's…there's no hard feelings."

Spade's thick-fingered right hand splayed itself against his chest. "I'm to have no hard feelings, too, is that it? About him jumping me in my own office?"

Her head lowered but her eyes sneaked up. "I said he was embarrassed. Can't you just…just wish us the best?"

"I wish you the best, Iva."

The widow rose. She got in her purse and came back with a slip of paper, which she pushed at him across the desk blotter. "Anyway, here's my new number. And address. If you ever…in case you want to know where to find me."

"That's fine, Iva. Goodbye."

"Goodbye, Sam.…Oh. I almost forgot."

Iva got into the purse again. "Here's Miles' office key."

She put it on Spade's desk.

He watched with a frozen smile as she went.

Then, after he heard the door onto the corridor close, he got up, scowling, and went out into the reception area.

Spade stood near Effie Perine's desk, thinking for a moment, and clapped once. He grinned and said: "Would you think less of me, angel, if I told you St. Nick just left me a present that tops them all—Iva Archer walking out of my life."

"Just a moment," his secretary said, but she wasn't talking to her boss. She covered the receiver with a red-nailed hand. "Someone would like to talk to you. It's a museum curator, he says."

"If his name is Blackwood, hang up."

"No, this is a real one."

She handed him the phone.

At the landscaped summit of the northwestern section of Lincoln Park stood San Francisco's grandest art gallery, the Palace of the Legion of Honor, a memorial to California's dead in the Great War.

The cream-colored building, with its porticos and rows of Ionic columns, replicated the French Pavilion at the 1915 Panama–Pacific International Exposition, itself patterned upon the Palais de la Légion d'Honneur in Paris. Among seventeenth-century French and Flemish tapestries, eighteenth-century

Italian, Dutch and English paintings, along with Rodin's sculpture *The Thinker*, a new acquisition was installed in March 1929 in the permanent collection and put on display under proper lighting in a glass case on a pedestal.

One of the museum's nineteen main-floor galleries, to the left and rear of the central foyer, was now home to a statuette of a falcon, solid gold and studded with jewels—rubies, diamonds, emeralds, amethysts, and sapphires—from crown to beak, from feathers to claw.

The object's label said: *The Maltese falcon is a gold and jewel-encrusted statuette sent as a tribute to Charles V of Spain by the Knights Templar of Malta in 1539.*

Gussied up by conservator-restorers, the fabulous statue drew crowds among whom heated discussions often broke out as to whether the gold statue itself was more valuable than the gems it sported.

Wanting to give the gawkers a chance to thin, Sam Spade and Effie Perine waited a few weeks before visiting their caged bird, shed of its black-lacquer skin.

The secretary, arm in arm with her boss, in their Sunday best, said, "I have to say I'm surprised and pleased that you made such a generous donation to the museum."

Spade's laugh was harsh. "Donation my eye. Gutman once offered me fifty grand for the damn thing, though he never ponied up more than ten. I settled for twenty-five, not from him but from some museum benefactor, then split ten between the real Corrine and the gambler. Held onto to the other fifteen, for the Spade agency coffers, lucky to get away with that."

"And your life," Effie reminded him.

"That too, angel. That too."

THE
END

SPADE WORK
Continuing Dashiell Hammett

I'm going to offer a few thoughts on why and how I went about writing *Return of the Maltese Falcon*. This is of course an optional read, and you are free to skip it with my thanks for picking this novel up.

But, before you go, I need to acknowledge a few books and their authors upon whose work I depended. Dashiell Hammett obviously towers over that list.

The 1961 paperback edition of *The Maltese Falcon* I read at age thirteen sported a Harry Bennett cover with Brigid O'Shaughnessy, Casper Gutman and Wilmer Cook portrayed in a then-modern manner. The publisher presented this great book as just another mystery novel, only twenty years after the John Huston film adaptation had been in theaters. I first saw Bogart's breakthrough movie on a Sunday morning when I skipped church by faking stomach flu.

Two of the novel's many editions were of enormous help to me here.

First, the Modern Library publication (1934) includes an introduction by Hammett, already not writing much anymore, which shares insights on how the novel derived from the writer's experiences as a private operative for the Pinkerton National Detective Agency, including suspects and other individuals he encountered on the job. He discussed reworking elements from short stories he felt hadn't lived up to their potential. The author also essentially admits writing *The Maltese*

Falcon without "the help of an outline or notes or even a clearly defined plot-idea in my head." The notion that this seminal tough mystery novel could have been, and apparently was, produced in a written-by-the-seat-of-the-pants fashion is frankly astonishing.

The other edition I depended upon comes from North Point Press, appropriately enough a San Francisco publisher; it's a handsome 1984 volume generously illustrated with full-page, mostly period, photos of the locations mentioned or implied in the novel. The twelve pages of end notes, printed in small footnote form, are packed with useful information. (The hardbound edition of the book grows increasingly pricey, but the trade paperback—its size and cover art identical to the hardcover—still can be found reasonably at this writing.)

I also read the somewhat different version of the novel's initial pulp serialization in editor Otto Penzler's *The Black Lizard Big Book of* Black Mask *Stories* (2010).

As a native Iowan who has visited San Francisco only a few times, I am no expert on the City by the Bay, so I was aided enormously by Don Herron's *The Dashiell Hammett Tour.* Mr. Herron conducts a by-appointment-tour that I have yet to take, but I feel as though I already have, thanks to his guidebook (thirtieth anniversary edition, 2009). This is an essential work for Hammett fans, beginning with a fine biography of the man and the writer, taking up a quarter of the book's pages, and worth the price of admission. Over the years, I have read every Hammett book-length biography I could find, and that's more than a few; but the guidebook's exceptional "brief" bio is the only one I referred to before I began (and during the writing of) this novel.

Like the North Point edition, the Herron guidebook is lavishly illustrated and written in an easygoing, accessible style as it delineates the various theories as to which locations are actually real ones. Hammett tends in *The Maltese Falcon* to rename the hotels but use the actual restaurants, sometimes thought to be the author trying to earn himself a free meal (a theory Herron dismisses). With its walking and driving maps, *The Dashiell Hammett Tour* is required reading for the Hammett enthusiast.

The bedrock of the research for my long-running Nathan Heller series has always been the WPA guides, not just for Nate's Chicago but the various cities he visits. The Heller novels put a private eye into the period in which the archetype for this sort of character was first created (largely by Hammett), and after which that character flourished in popular culture, a context in which my protagonist investigates real, often famous unsolved (or controversially solved) cases. It's hard to imagine being able to write those books without the American Guide Series, and that also proved to be the case with *Return of the Maltese Falcon. California: A Guide to the Golden State* (1939) and *San Francisco: The Bay and Its Cities* (1940) were predictably helpful. Mystery fiction authority J. Kingston Pierce—knowing I was setting out to write this novel—generously sent me his excellent book, *San Francisco: Yesterday and Today* (2009), which proved most helpful as well.

That said, any inaccuracies and inconsistencies regarding the geography of San Francisco here are my own.

I chose not to revisit the film versions of *The Maltese Falcon*—the 1931 feature directed by Roy Del Ruth, somewhat forgotten today; a loose remake, *Satan Met a Lady*, in 1936; and then of course the classic John Huston-directed masterpiece in 1941—or any more recent works inspired by the book. (Joe Gores, a fine mystery writer and like Hammett a real-life private eye in his younger days, wrote a prequel novel titled *Spade & Archer* in 2009. A 2023 AMC television series, *Monsieur Spade*, apparently relocated the character to France.) My novel is strictly a continuation of Hammett's original and does not incorporate elements introduced in any later adaptation (or in Hammett's own later writings, for that matter). In writing this novel, I did not wish to be influenced in any way by anything other than *The Maltese Falcon* as readers first encountered it back in 1929.

To any who may think I am a buzzard picking at the *Falcon*'s bones, I can only say this is a novel I dreamed of doing for many years, and have been keeping an eye on the clock (as it were) as to the original's public-domain status. I am something of an old hand at working in the vineyards of creators I admire, having taken over the writing of the *Dick Tracy* comic strip from Chester Gould for fifteen years, and finishing various works-in-progress of Mickey Spillane, including fourteen Mike Hammer novels, fulfilling the writer's request of me in his last days.

My fascination with the work of Dashiell Hammett, Raymond Chandler and Mickey Spillane goes back, again, to around 1961. Two TV series sparked this trend—*Peter Gunn* (1959–1961) and *77 Sunset Strip* (1958–1964)—though two series preceding those lit the fuse (*Perry Mason*, 1957–1966; and *Mickey Spillane's Mike Hammer*, 1957–1959).

As an adolescent and then a young teenager caught up in those shows, I was aware that many, even most, of them had literary roots. Erle Stanley Gardner, Raymond Chandler, and Mickey Spillane had TV series derived from their popular books; even *77 Sunset Strip* came from television giant Roy Huggins having started out as a Chandler imitator with a Stuart Bailey novel (*The Double Take*, 1946) and three novellas (collected as *77 Sunset Strip*, 1959). Though not credited on screen, this video afterlife is true of Dashiell Hammett as well, with the Peter Lawford-Phyllis Kirk-starring *The Thin Man*, 1957–1959.

My tendency in those days, and to a degree now, was to look

at the literary source of any movie or television show that had caught my attention. When I was 13, that impulse is what led me to Hammett, Chandler and Spillane, the three writers who—in their respective decades—defined the private eye in popular culture.

Among the things that fascinated me then, and still does, is how different these three writers are in their approach and style. Hammett with his characters the Continental Op and Sam Spade is a former trained operative who brought a terse, informed eye to the crime story; Chandler, raised in Great Britain, with his slightly tarnished knight Phillip Marlowe raised first-person narration to a level only rivaled by Mark Twain in *Adventures of Huckleberry Finn* (1884); and Spillane brought a rough-hewn pulp energy inspired by Hammett's *Black Mask* magazine contemporary, Carroll John Daly, to new heights of popularity (and new depths of controversy).

What I have attempted to do in *Return of the Maltese Falcon* is honor the original novel and its author without writing strictly pastiche—allowing some of my native style to creep in while honoring the original's.

When I reread *The Maltese Falcon* with writing this novel in mind—designing it more as a continuation than a sequel—I was surprised to see how subjective the Spade-centric omniscient narrator is. The objectivity of Hammett's refusal to go into the point of view of his characters, including (especially) Sam Spade himself, is what makes the author's approach so distinctive. He had written the Continental Op stories and two novels in the first person, after all; and only his later three (and unfortunately final) novels employ that technique, though some non-Spade short stories use it as well. This observation was freeing to me.

I also allowed myself, to a certain degree, to do more place description than Hammett. On some level, *Return of the Maltese*

Falcon is a historical novel, or at the very least a period one. This hopes to honor Hammett's style as well as stay faithful to the period in which the original was written—for example, women are often called "girls" and Sam Spade smokes to an alarming extent. To maintain a sense of the continuity with the original novel, I attempted as much as possible to operate within Spade's world—the places he inhabits and goes, as well as the characters he meets, sometimes characters mentioned in Hammett appearing on stage for the first time.

Among Hammett's stylistic quirks that I have followed is a tendency to always call certain characters—primarily female ones—by their full first and last names. He also frequently uses colons and not commas after "said"—I do this occasionally here myself. It's part of what's commonly thought of as Hammett's terse style, but a writer who starts a novel with the omniscient narrator describing the protagonist as looking "rather pleasantly like a blond satan" isn't really all that objective.

Sam Spade's impact on popular culture and the private eye genre is remarkable considering the character only appears in one novel and three short stories. John Huston's enduring film, with its iconic cast, cannot be underestimated in having extended Spade's impact. But the character also went on to headline *The Adventures of Sam Spade* (1946–1951), an enormously popular radio show, as spoofy as *The Maltese Falcon* was straight. The money that series and *The Adventures of the Thin Man* (1941–1950) made, plus that of the Hammett-created *The Fat Man* (1946–1951), a combination of Sydney Greenstreet's Casper Gutman and the Continental Op, freed Hammett from the need to make a living from his fiction, as did income from film adaptations.

It's my hope that readers—frustrated by this great writer only giving us five novels, and no further Sam Spade ones—will enjoy and accept this effort as a kind of love letter to Dashiell Hammett and the private eye form.

Before I go, I need to thank a few people. I took this project to Andrew Sumner at Titan Books, who was a booster and later editor of the Mike Hammer novels I completed from the partial Spillane novels-in-progress left behind at Mickey's passing. Andrew brought my proposal and synopsis to Titan publishers Nick Landau and Vivian Cheung, who suggested taking it to their sister company, Hard Case Crime. Under the HCC editorship of Charles Ardai, I've written any number of books, including reviving my Quarry series and continuing the Nathan Heller saga, among other things. Charles is a good friend with a fine instinct for hardboiled/*noir* fiction. Thank you, too, to my friend and agent Dominick Abel.

Finally, my in-house editor and collaborator (as "Barbara Allan"), Barbara Collins has been particularly invaluable on this one. Thank you, angel.

MAX ALLAN COLLINS was named a Grand Master in 2017 by the Mystery Writers of America. He is a three-time winner of the Private Eye Writers of America's Shamus Award, as well as their Life Achievement award, the Eye (2006). His graphic novel *Road to Perdition* (1998) became the Academy Award-winning film directed by Sam Mendes and starring Tom Hanks. His other comics credits include the syndicated strip *Dick Tracy*, *Batman*, and (with artist Terry Beatty) his own *Ms. Tree* and *Wild Dog*. He has completed fourteen Mike Hammer novels begun by the late Mickey Spillane, and his Hammer audio novel *The Little Death* with Stacy Keach won a 2011 Audie. Recently he adapted the first of his Nathan Heller novels into a ten-part audio drama, *True Noir*.

For five years, he was sole licensing writer for TV's *CSI: Crime Scene Investigation*, creating best-selling novels, graphic novels, and video games. His movie tie-in novels have appeared on the *USA Today* and *New York Times* bestseller lists, including *Saving Private Ryan*, *Air Force One*, and *American Gangster*.

Max has written and directed two documentaries and seven feature films, including the Lifetime movie *Mommy* (1996); and he scripted *The Expert*, a 1995 HBO World Premiere, as well as the film-festival favorite *The Last Lullaby* (2009) based on his innovative Quarry novels, which were also adapted as a 2016 TV series by Cinemax, for which Max wrote two scripts. Collins properties have also been optioned by Skydance, Lionsgate and CBS Films. His most recent self-scripted/directed indie films are *Mickey Spillane's Encore for Murder* (2022), *Blue Christmas* (2023) and *Death by Fruitcake* (2024).

A lifelong resident of Muscatine, Iowa, Max co-writes the Antiques "Trash 'n' Treasures" mysteries with his wife Barbara. Their son Nathan is a Japanese-to-English translator with credits including the novel *Battle Royale* and the manga *JoJo's Bizarre Adventure*.

From the Author of

RETURN of the MALTESE FALCON

Try These Other Novels From
MAX ALLAN COLLINS...

The Big Bundle

Private eye Nathan Heller investigates the kidnaping of a millionaire's son being held for the highest ransom ever paid.

Too Many Bullets

Nathan Heller is on duty when presidential candidate Robert F. Kennedy is assassinated. Can he unravel the web of deception surrounding the killer...?

The First Quarry

A professional killer's first assignment: murder a philandering professor who has run afoul of some very dangerous men.

Read On for a Sample Chapter From
THE BIG BUNDLE!

ONE

A middle-aged man taking stock of his life is to be expected. But for this to be my midpoint, I would have to make it to 94, and anyway it was the ghosts of my past haunting me, not my conscience, which after all was the nine millimeter Browning automatic I still carried all these years after my father killed himself with it—when I disappointed him taking the Outfit's money to get ahead on the Chicago PD.

As I write this I'm closer to 94 than 47, which was my age in October 1953 when I caught an Ace Company cab outside the Kansas City Municipal Airport. The cabbie was colored, which in a city where the population was 10% that persuasion might not have been a surprise. Still, Negro hackies didn't generally work white areas, though airport runs could make for a decent fare and those who didn't like the driver's shade could take the next ride down, and those who didn't give a damn got a smile and a nod and no funny business like unrequested tours of K.C.

And I didn't need one of those—I'd done jobs here before. The airport was five minutes from a downtown whose "Petticoat Lane" on Eleventh Street had smart shops and patrons who could afford to frequent them; around Twelfth and Main were the usual stores and palatial movie houses, a few blocks east was a civic center whose plaza included two of the taller buildings, the Courthouse and City Hall, with the massive bunker of Municipal Auditorium to the southeast.

Everything was still up to date in Kansas City. They were giving my toddling town a run on the meat-packing and agricultural fronts. They had an impressive art gallery, fine arts museum and kiddie-pleasing zoo, and the industries included steel, petroleum, and automotive manufacturing. And one once-booming local enterprise that had faded since the '30s had made a big comeback recently.

"You in town about that kidnapping, boss?" the cabbie asked.

He was grinning at me in the rearview mirror. He looked like Mantan Moreland but with a flattened nose; that and his cauliflower ears made him a former prizefighter. Yes, I'm a detective.

"Why would you think that?"

Now he was looking out his windshield, which was my preference.

"Address rang a bell," he said.

"Ah."

"Anyway, boss, I read about you—you that private eye to the stars."

Life magazine had done a story about me when I opened my L.A. branch.

"Don't recall your name, though," he said.

"Nathan Heller," I said.

"Chicago, right?"

"Right."

"...So what's Alan Ladd like?"

"Short."

"What about Mitchum?"

"Tall."

That made him laugh.

For the record, I was an inch shorter than Mitchum and weighed around two hundred pounds, my reddish brown hair going white at the temples, and "almost leading man handsome" (the *Life* writer had said). I made up for the "almost" by being a success in my trade—president of Chicago's A-1 Detective

Agency. By way of evidence I offer the court my Botany 500 suit, Dobbs hat and Burberry raincoat, lining in—it was cold in Kansas City in October, and the sky was trying to make its mind up whether to rain or snow.

We rumbled across the Missouri River by way of the upper deck of the Hannibal Bridge.

No laughter now, as he asked, "You gonna help get that little boy back?"

"Do my best."

"I got a boy that age myself."

"So do I."

"I believe somebody took *my* boy, I kill his ass."

"So would I."

He laughed again, but the sound of it was different.

Just under a week ago, a bit before nine A.M., someone rang the bell at an exclusive Catholic elementary school here in Kansas City. A young, inexperienced nun answered and found a plump, pleasant-looking (though agitated) woman on the doorstep; about forty, the caller looked respectable enough in a brown hat, beige blouse and dark gabardine skirt. The woman even wore white gloves.

She presented herself as the sister of Virginia Greenlease, whose six-year-old son Bobby attended the school, and said she'd just rushed her sister, who'd shown signs of a heart attack while they were out shopping, to the hospital. Virginia was asking to see her son. The nun—new at the school, barely speaking English—fetched the child and turned him over to the woman calling herself the boy's aunt. The boy went along dutifully, hand-in-hand.

Later that morning the mother superior's second-in-command called the Greenlease home to check on how Mrs. Greenlease was feeling.

Mrs. Greenlease, who answered the phone herself, said, "Why, just fine."

The first ransom letter came a few hours later, special delivery.

We moved through an industrial area and then an unpretentious mix of commercial and residential, all pretty sleepy on an early Sunday afternoon. In the plush Country Club District, broad, winding boulevards followed the contours of the terrain, interrupted by public areas overseen by sculptures and fountains; a classy retail plaza ran to Spanish-style stucco and cream-color brick. The homes themselves were near mansions—not just "near," really—with impeccably landscaped, evergreen-garnished yards that in warmer weather were likely trimmed about as often as their owners saw their barbers.

"We in Kansas now, Mr. Heller."

We'd only been traveling fifteen minutes. "Over the state line already?"

"Yessir. This is Mission Hills. Lots of rich folks. You a golfer, sir?"

"I am." I disliked the sport, but sometimes it was the best way to keep clients happy.

"Well, they's three golf courses to choose from. They keep 'em open till the first snow."

Autumn had turned the plentiful trees into a riot of color, orange, yellow, red, green, even purple, that last desperate burst of life before winter delivered death. But the grass was still green, brown barely intruding, with a scattering of those vivid colors making a patchwork quilt of lawns. Fathers were tossing footballs to sons while littler kids leapt into heaping piles of leaves with a fearlessness they'd yet to outgrow, their mothers leaning on rakes and looking on in worried surrender.

The cab was about to turn onto Verona Road from West 63rd when a figure in a fedora and raincoat ambled out from around the corner and planted himself before us with his arms outstretched. The cabbie hadn't been traveling fast in this residential area, but it was startling enough to make him hit the brakes with a squeal.

Tall, his long, narrow oval face home to a prominent nose and jutting chin, eyebrows heavy on a high forehead, the interloper came over to the window the cabbie was rolling down and leaned in like an officious carhop.

"Local traffic only," he said, polite but with an edge.

I leaned up and said to the cabbie, "I'll handle this."

I got out and said, "Nathan Heller. They're expecting me at the Greenlease home."

"Special Agent Wesley Grapp," he said, stepping away from the cab, holding up ID with his left hand and offering his right with the slightest of smiles. His grip was firm but not showy. "You're on our list."

I gave him about half a grin. "I've been on the FBI's list a long time."

That got a chuckle out of him. "Yes, I've seen the file. It's thicker than *Forever Amber* and about as juicy. What did you do to get on the Chief's bad side? It's not included."

The Chief, of course, was J. Edgar Hoover.

"Oh," I said casually, "a long time ago I told him to go fuck himself."

This chuckle came from somewhere deep. "That'll do it. Call me Wes."

"And I'm Nate. So you've set up a checkpoint."

"We have. We'll take you from here."

My overnight bag was in the trunk and the cabbie got it out for me. I gave him a sawbuck and made a friend for life.

Grapp walked me around the corner to his ride, a dark blue Ford Crestliner. I tossed the bag in front where a younger agent in suit and fedora sat behind the wheel—slender in horn-rimmed glasses—and Grapp and I got in back.

I said, "I guess you know Bob Greenlease called me in personally. You have no objection?"

"None. I'm all for it, actually."

That surprised me; the FBI didn't usually welcome private detectives to the party. "Why's that?"

"We've been pretty well frozen out of this so far. Helping as much as we're allowed. Mr. Greenlease has kept us pretty much at arm's length. The guy's got a lot of clout. He's working strictly through the K.C. chief of police."

Greenlease, a major stockholder in General Motors, was one of the wealthiest men in the Midwest. A self-made man from farming stock, he'd started out around the turn of the century making handmade cars and running a repair garage, then landed a franchise to sell Cadillacs; now he was the largest distributor of Caddies in the Southwest. His founding dealership, the Greenlease Motor Car Company, was where I first met him in 1937, when I was brought in to deal with auto parts pilfering by employees. And since just after the war, the A-1 had arranged security for the Annual Chicago Automobile Show, of which Greenlease was always a big part.

"Of course FBI policy in kidnapping cases," Grapp was saying, "means doing nothing that might jeopardize the victim's safe return. And Mr. Greenlease insists on no surveillance of any ransom drop…or at least he has so far."

"So far?"

"Well, Mr. Heller…Nate…he's called *you* in. Might mean a change of tactics."

"Yeah, but it's taken almost a week." I'd half expected a call; the case had made the papers and even CBS-TV by way of Edward R. Murrow's fifteen-minute national evening news.

But that had amounted to little more than descriptions of the boy and the fake aunt. And expressions of ongoing sympathy for the parents.

"We don't have a man on the inside," Grapp said. "So your cooperation could prove key."

"What *have* you been able to do?"

He offered me a smoke and I declined. He lit up and said, "With Kansas and Missouri butting up against each other, chances are good this thing has crossed state lines, which'll give us jurisdiction. Already we've been able to intercept Greenlease's mail at the K.C. Post Office and record incoming phone calls."

"So there's been contact. Were you able to trace the calls?"

He sighed smoke. "We probably could have, and possibly closed in on the people responsible, but the family's wish was that we do nothing that might hinder the boy's return."

I frowned, shook my hand. "That's crazy."

"I agree. Perhaps you can reason with Mr. Greenlease. After all, he's taken a big step, bringing you in…considering your reputation."

"Somehow I don't think you mean to flatter me."

A thick eyebrow went up. "Nate. Mr. Heller. You're well-known for your underworld connections. And you've been in a number of well-publicized situations where you have, let's say, taken matters effectively into hand."

"Gee whiz, thanks. But let me remind you, Wes, Special Agent Grapp, that J. Edgar Hoover assures us that there is no such thing as organized crime."

The young agent at the wheel frowned at me in the rearview mirror, but Grapp only smiled a little.

He gestured with the cigarette-in-hand. "Nate, let's just say anything you can do to help this situation would be appreciated. Whoever did this goddamn thing must be aware that, even if state lines *haven't* been crossed, the kidnapping law in Missouri means a death sentence."

"Understood. Since there's effectively been a press blackout, what can you tell me? What don't I know?"

The FBI man's laugh was raspy and wry. "You have been spared experiencing one of the most sadistic, heartless series of letters and messages and phone calls any of us has ever seen. Six ransom notes, over a dozen phone calls. One wild goose chase after another." His eyes, a dark brown and almost black, narrowed. "We do know they have the boy, or at least *had* him—a medal he'd worn to school that day was sent along with the second note."

"When you say 'they'...?"

"It's at least two people. The woman who picked the boy up at school, and a man who's been making the phone calls. He insists Bobby's still alive. Talks about him being a handful and mentions a pet the child misses, how homesick he is. But, uh... they aren't the smartest pair, these two."

"Why do you say that?"

"Well, they were lucky they snagged the kid at all. The nun who answered the door was new, very young, an import from France who spoke little English, and if the mother superior—away on an errand—had been there to go to the door that morning? That damn woman would *never* have pulled off her impersonation."

"Think so, huh?"

He nodded curtly. "When the nun offered to show her the way to the chapel, to pray for her sick sibling? The dumbo dame said, 'No thanks, I'm not a Catholic.' Any other nun in that facility would've known that Mrs. Greenlease was a Catholic, meaning her sister would be, too!"

I let some air out. "That makes the woman a dope. But maybe the guy's got more on the ball."

"You think so, Heller? His first ransom note? He got the address wrong."

They drove me down Verona Road, past a trio of cars with PRESS cards in the rear windows; a TV camera truck was pulled over there, too. A female reporter was using a phone in a box strapped to a tree, a little stool next to it for her purse and whatnot. United Press International had installed the phone, Grapp said.

The press had a good view of the house from there. Of course, "house" didn't cover it. An imposing two-story multi-gabled structure with slate roofs and a cream-and-brown field-stone facade awaited us when we pulled in the half-circle drive; it was almost a castle and not quite a church, and wide enough to be a hotel.

The FBI dropped me off and I toted my overnight bag to the gabled entrance. I must have been watched from a window, because the door opened after I'd barely rung the bell. In his mid-thirties, my host was of average height and weight with a squared-off head and a rounded jaw, his forehead so high it was like his features had slipped down too far on his oval face. His hair was dark and short, his eyes dark and bloodshot, his dark suit and tie unusual for a Sunday afternoon, unless an evening church service was in the mix. Yet somehow he still seemed disheveled.

"You must be Mr. Heller," he said, and stepped aside and gestured me in. He took my coat, hat and bag and set them on a chair by a mirror.

Then I was in a world of big rooms with dark woodwork, pale plaster walls, dark wood floors, tall leaded-glass windows; along the left wall, a stairway rose with a carved lion for a newel post. The interior seemed oddly at war with itself—everything Prairie-style and spare but for carved touches, as if the house couldn't decide if it was a mission or a manor.

Few lights were on. This was a somber place—not necessarily always so, but right now the inhabitants could not quite acknowledge light, which even the tall windows seemed reluctant to admit.

He was about to lead me deeper into the house when he froze, remembering himself, and turned and said, with a stiff nod, "Paul Greenlease."

This was the adopted son of Bob Greenlease's first marriage; Greenlease's second wife, Virginia, had presented her husband with two late-in-life children, a daughter whose name I didn't recall and of course the missing Bobby.

"I've been serving as the family's spokesman," Paul said, offering a listless handshake. "Dad has taken this awfully hard."

We were standing in an entryway larger than most living rooms.

"I'm sure," I said. "How's your mother doing?"

"It kind of varies, day to day. She's been sedated a lot, frankly. Sometimes things seem to be looking up, then…"

"Then they're down. I understand these creatures have you folks jumping through hoops—one message, one call, one snipe hunt after another."

He nodded, swallowed. "They've left us notes under crayon-marked rocks. They've taped letters underneath mailboxes. One note sent us to another note with instructions too confusing to follow."

"Sounds like you're dealing with dolts."

He had an ashen look. "They want a lot of money. That's not a problem, understand, but it took a while to get together."

"How much?"

He paused, not sure he should share this, then did: "Six hundred thousand. Dollars."

"Good God. That must be a record."

"I wouldn't know. Is that a lot for this kind of thing?"

Lindbergh had been asked for $50,000. Of course that was a while ago. Inflation had hit every business.

"The very first letter specified federal reserve notes," Paul said, "in tens and twenties. Mr. Eisenhower at Commerce Trust is helping. He's the president's brother."

"Of the bank?"

"No, of America. You know—Ike?"

"Yeah." I didn't mention I hadn't voted for him. "And Ike's brother got the money together?"

"Yes. And we tried to deliver it but it was raining and these letters have been kind of illiterate and…well, we left the money but the kidnapper called us later and said he couldn't find it."

Jesus.

"We went back and picked the money up," Paul said, escorting me down a hallway. "We tried another time, but….You should really talk to my father."

We stopped at a doorless archway. Very softly, he said, "Sue's become a sort of appendage to Dad. She's eleven. They're sort of…helping each other through this."

"I understand."

"But it might hamper what gets said. Just so you know."

"Got it."

We moved through the archway into a big living room. Again, the room was fighting itself, stark Arts and Crafts furnishings, walls of square-panel mahogany, but a ceiling of ornate plaster work with a chandelier; a grand piano lurked in one corner, the fireplace going, dispensing warmth out of a coldly elaborate decorative mantel over which hung a gilt-framed painting, a family portrait of Robert Greenlease and his wife Virginia with a much younger Paul at his side and a toddler Sue by her mother's. Bobby Greenlease, not yet born, was already absent.

A dark leather-cushioned Stickley sofa faced the fire and the back of Robert Greenlease's head and his broad shoulders—he was in a blue satin dressing gown—were to me.

"Dad," Paul said quietly from where we stood just inside the room, "Mr. Heller from Chicago is here."

Greenlease's hand raised slowly, like a slow child risking an answer in class, and he gently motioned me forward. He did not turn.

Paul nodded to me and disappeared and I went around to face Greenlease, who wore a white shirt and tie under the dressing gown, its lapels so dark blue they were almost black. His eleven-year-old daughter, blonde and cute in a plaid jumper, was curled up sleeping next to him on a brown leather sofa cushion, her head on his knee; his hand was on her shoulder.

In his early seventies, Bob Greenlease was a big man with a rectangular head and white hair, wispy on top. His eyes were wide-set and light blue behind browline glasses, nose hawkish, mouth a thin line, a face that could have been severe but wasn't, because he so frequently smiled.

Of course he wasn't smiling now.

Seated or not, he had an off-balance look, as if he'd just realized he stood at the edge of a cliff.

He whispered, "Thank you for coming, Nate. We'll keep our voices down. Don't want to disturb the girl."

He extended his left hand—his right remaining on his daughter's shoulder—and we awkwardly but warmly shook.

I drew up a wood-and-leather-cushion chair, careful not to let it screech on the hardwood floor. "I'm so sorry about this terrible thing," I said, sotto voce.

"Your son is well? Sam, isn't it?"

"Yes. With his mother in California. He's six. Like your boy."

The tight mouth flinched. "Wish I'd called you in sooner.

Should have been smart enough to take advantage of your prior experience with Lindbergh and all."

I knew what he meant. But I wondered how it made me an expert, considering how that had come out.

I said, "You don't have to fill me in. I spoke to Agent Grapp and your son and heard all about this damn nonsense you've had to endure."

He nodded, just barely. "We seem to finally be on the verge of arranging the ransom drop. It's been like something out of the Marx Brothers. But we're to get a phone call at eight P.M. with the instructions."

The fire snapped at us and was almost too warm as it cast an orange glow.

"What do you want me to do, Bob?"

"Join the team. Two old friends of mine, valued business associates, have been helping out on this thing—Will Letterman, who runs my Tulsa dealership, and from my K.C. operation here, Stew O'Neill. You'll meet them. Fine fellas."

"I'm sure they are. But you're obviously dealing with dangerous, unscrupulous criminals. You need someone who can handle that breed."

His smile was barely discernible. "Which is why I wish I'd called you sooner. Are you too old and successful, Nate, to still carry that Browning semiautomatic pistol?"

I nodded toward the outer area. "It's in my bag. Holster, too."

"Good. Afraid we don't have room for you here, between the help and my support crew. I've had arrangements made for you at the Hotel President, just fifteen minutes away. I've got a new Cadillac waiting for your use, here in the garage—Paul has keys for you. Go get settled at the hotel and be back at seven-thirty. I'll introduce you to Will and Stew."

"Fine." I got to my feet. "How are you holding up?"

"A lot of support here. Good people. My son and Will have been handling the press. My daughter sticks right by me, and my wife…well, Virginia has occasional rough moments, but she's smart and strong. She took the call that came in today, herself, and let this 'M'…that's what he calls himself…have it."

"Really."

"Yes. Told the bastard there'd been enough runaround. But afterward…" He swallowed thickly and the blue eyes behind the glasses were glittering. "…she rather…came apart. You see, she had specific questions that M couldn't, or anyway didn't, answer. Name of our driver on the latest European trip…what Bobby was building with his monkey blocks in his room. The caller skated over those, just said what a handful Bobby was being. I think for the first time, Virginia…well. You know."

I did know. She had realized how possible it was that her boy might already be dead.

The little girl stirred. She looked up at me with big eyes, as blue as her father's, and grabbed his arm, startled, afraid. "Is he one of them, Daddy?"

"No, darling. This is Mr. Heller. He's on our side."